Remember when

LINDSAY DETWILER

Remember When © 2017 by Lindsay Detwiler

Remember When is a work of fiction. All names, characters, events and places found therein are either from the author's imagination or used fictitiously. Any similarity to persons alive or dead, actual events, locations, or organizations is entirely coincidental and not intended by the author.

For information, contact the publisher, Hot Tree Publishing.

www.hottreepublishing.com

Editing: Hot Tree Editing

Cover Designer: Claire Smith

Formatter: RMGraphX

ISBN-10: 1-925448-85-1

ISBN-13: 978-1-925448-85-6

10 9 8 7 6 5 4 3 2 1

To my husband,
I will love you until my dying breath,
and to Henry,
my best friend.

Forward

When you're gone from this place, what will be left behind? What will remain in this world to tell your story?

A newspaper? Some photographs? Your children? A journal?

Will these items or people be able to capture you? Will they tell of the times you loved, the times you lost, and all the moments in between? Will they capture the laughs, smiles, and heartaches? Will they capture the times you danced in the rain and sang in the shower and laughed so hard for no reason?

When you're gone from this place, will your story really be left behind, or will it disappear?

Forward

Prologue

NAME: JESSICA KLING
DOB: 2/27/1988
CAUSE OF DEATH: ?

The words swirled like a demonic carousel in her mind, a restless cycle. They whirled and taunted, the only things left in her mind, frozen like the rest of her body. She tilted her head to the right, her gaze appraising Todd. The simple movement was tedious, sucking up every last ounce of energy she had. Her cyclical, morbid thoughts about what the report would say halted.

Todd was slipping away. He didn't have much longer to hang on. In truth, neither did she.

This wasn't how it was supposed to be. This wasn't where their story was supposed to end. There was so much left to do, so much left unfinished. She didn't want the question mark filled in with starvation or dehydration or pneumonia or hypothermia or whatever else they could use to fill in the blank. These days, the choices were plentiful.

She wanted to leave her cause of death a question. She wanted to leave the mystery for another day, preferably one decades down the road. She wanted to explore life, to finish her bucket list, to simply bask in the normalcy of day-to-day living she'd taken for granted. She wanted to finish out their love story, to make more memories with him. She didn't want this to be the final severance of their relationship, the eternal end.

"T-t-odd?" she stammered, her voice cracking, her words almost inaudible.

He didn't respond.

"T-t-odd," she said again, this time moving her arm to touch him, the movement also difficult.

A groan escaped from his lips.

"Todd, you can't… sleep…. Not now."

Silence. Bone-chilling silence.

And then, finally, a mumble, words crackling. "I'm… h-here. I'm s-still—" He coughed, the last words cut off by a guttural sputtering deep in the recesses of his lungs.

The words, even ignoring the cough, weren't reassuring. They weren't the words of a man reaffirming his hold on life, his will to survive.

They were the desperate words of a man giving up, of a man checking out, of a man tossing hope aside.

She wanted to cry, but she couldn't. She was too hungry, too thirsty, too tired, and too cold to cry. She'd done enough of that. She kept staring at him, the man who had been her rock. The man she wanted to grow old with. The man she'd pledged her life to.

Her heart cracked inside her chest as one debilitating question surfaced in her mind, usurping all other emotions and thoughts: Was this really how it would all end?

Chapter One

THREE DAYS EARLIER
NIGHT ONE

"Will you *please* turn down the radio? I can't focus when you're singing so loudly." She gripped the steering wheel so tightly, her knuckles were probably pure white underneath the cotton fabric of her gloves. They'd been driving for a half hour, and the truck's heat finally warmed the interior, clearing away her icy breath. She blinked hard, her contacts sticking to her eyes, her night vision playing tricks on her. The snow hypnotized her. It flashed in front of the windshield, pelting against it diagonally in haphazard patterns. She took a deep breath, trying to calm herself.

"But baby, it's my song," Todd teased. She didn't respond, so he obliged. "Hey," he said into the darkness. "We're going to be okay. Just breathe. You're doing great."

He sounded like a labor and delivery room coach instead of a passenger during what was practically a blizzard at midnight.

"You know I hate night driving."

"Pull over, then. I'll take the wheel."

"You were drinking."

"I had two beers. Five hours ago. It'll be fine."

She considered it. She didn't know why she'd agreed to drive in the first place. She hated driving—sucked at it, really. It still made her nervous as hell to be behind the wheel. But she'd thought Todd deserved a night to drink a little, kick back, especially since he didn't know anyone at the wedding. So she'd agreed to drive, jumping in the seat on the way out of the banquet hall, trying to talk down her nerves.

"I'll just keep going."

Silence invaded as Jessica focused on the road, Todd quiet, probably tired from the hectic day. She felt like she'd run a marathon, all of the excitement fading. She couldn't wait to be back home, cuddled in their bed by the fireplace, the television set at a low murmur to whisk her to sleep. She planned on skipping church the next day to spend the morning languidly lounging in Todd's arms. She'd make waffles and try not to burn them this time. They'd have a few cups of coffee, lounge around with Henry, and recover from today before returning to work for another week of drudgery.

They had to get home first. The snow intensified, quickly covering the road, painting over the yellow lines. The wind, howling and powerful, only made the situation worse, beating against the metal door of the truck. Luckily, they hadn't brought her pathetic excuse for a car. It would've probably been stuck in the snow already, or picked up into a cloud in the heavy winds.

"We should've left after the bridal dance," Todd said calmly, not accusing her but just observing.

"You know we couldn't. Erica's one of my best friends."

"Who you don't even talk to anymore," Todd replied. Jess's defenses rose.

"We talk."

"Once a year?"

"Shut up. We're busy. She's still my friend, though. I couldn't just bail. Plus, we had fun. It was good to be out. You didn't seem to be complaining too much when you were dancing to the 'YMCA,' you know."

"I know, I know. But I told you it was supposed to get bad. We really should've left earlier."

"I thought you were exaggerating. I thought you just wanted to get home early to play some *Fallout 4*."

"Well, I mean, I'm always up for that. But have you been living under a rock? They're calling for storm system after storm system. It's supposed to snow a ton for days on end. We're under a winter storm warning now, for Christ's sake, woman."

"Don't call me woman. You know I hate that," she said, but smiled in spite of herself.

"Oh, yeah. You really hate it so much." He snickered, and she shook her head. Despite his annoying comments, she found herself calming down. Todd did that for her.

"Just another two hours and we'll be home," she

announced, taking one hand off the wheel to adjust her scratchy formalwear. Her legs were cold, even with the lined tights she had on and the heat blasting. She returned her hand to the wheel, tapping to the song, trying to reassure herself.

"Who the hell gets married this time of year?" Todd complained, also tapping on the dashboard to the now low-volume music.

"Shut up," she said, teasing. He was such a sarcastic jerk sometimes.

She struggled to keep her eyes open as exhaustion crept in. The day had been long. Fun, but long. What *had* they been thinking? At the time, driving home a few hours at midnight seemed like no big deal. They hadn't wanted to get a hotel room because of Henry; she worried he'd be lonely staying home all night by himself. Plus, it would save money to just drive home. She hadn't, however, planned on staying at the wedding so late. Now it seemed like a ridiculous idea. They should've just stayed in a hotel. Todd's mom would've kept Henry if they'd just asked.

Or they should've just sent back the RSVP card with a "no" checked on it and called it a day. She didn't want to admit it, but Todd was sort of right. Erica wasn't really close to her anymore. Life and distance had tossed a wedge between them. Erica probably wouldn't have even noticed if Jess hadn't been there. It's not like it would've completely ruined her day.

Still, it felt like the right thing to do. If nothing else, then to honor the friendship they'd once had. Plus, she loved weddings. She loved the magic of it. She loved remembering her own special day, the butterflies and the feeling that life had forever changed. She loved how she got to walk into weddings now with the man who caused those butterflies.

Todd kept tapping energetically on the dashboard, humming along with the song. She smiled to herself, shaking her head. Despite his terrible singing voice and sometimes annoying remarks, she loved him. God, did she love him. Sitting beside him during the ceremony just stirred those butterflies in her again. She couldn't imagine her life without him.

Not that things were perfect. God knew he drove her crazy. *Freaking crazy.* Socks scattered around the bedroom, cereal in the sink. His tendency to leave empty snack boxes in the pantry. His sometimes too free-spirited nature. His ability to not see the weeds growing up through the deck. His need to be constantly reminded that Thursdays were trash day. His loud singing to every song on the radio. His teasing attitude.

Their marriage was, like many, dented and tainted by imperfection. There were moments of fury, of frustration, of undeniable exhaustion. They poked and prodded at each other's weaknesses, and sometimes they pushed each other away. They, like all couples, went to bed angry. They said horrible things in the middle of raging, inferno-like fights. They were far from perfect, for sure.

Still, in moments like this, Todd tapping out an Usher song while he tried to take her mind off her treacherous fear, she remembered it didn't matter. Perfection didn't matter. Being with him was all that did.

"Just a couple of hours," she mumbled again, chanting it to make herself believe all was well. The tires had skidded and slid a few times, but with no cars on the road near them, it was all good. Even if she did lose control a little bit, it would be fine. She'd just take her time, limp the truck home, and they'd be tucked away in bed before she knew it.

The desolation was a blessing but also a little eerie. The emptiness of the road; the area devoid of life. The wedding had been, quite literally, in the middle of nowhere, a backcountry kind of hoedown in a rustic barn. Good thing she'd filled up on gas on the way, because there was nowhere to stop now until they were closer to home.

"A couple of hours? Not at this speed," Todd teased, snapping her back to the present. He pretended to throw his head back in boredom, groaning loudly.

"I prefer to get us home in one piece," she retorted, turning to look at him. He just winked at her.

The snow ricocheted off the windshield. She pushed the gas down a touch more, just to prove her point that she was capable. She wanted to shut him up. More than that, she did want to be home. Emboldened by the empty road in front of her and Todd's teasing, she settled in the seat, relaxing her grip on the wheel. They'd driven through worse than this. They'd be home before things got really bad. It was fine.

The truck swerved, and Jess's heart panged a bit, stripping away her boost of confidence. She eased off the gas a little bit to straighten the situation out, then slowly applied more pressure again.

"That's ice, babe. Slow down," Todd said, seriousness creeping in. "I really think maybe you should let me drive."

"You just told me I was driving too slow."

"Yeah, but I didn't mean for you to go all Evel Knievel

on me."

She kept her eyes on the road, taking in the scene. If she weren't terrified, she'd think it was pretty. The snow piled all around, the snow and ice crackling against the windshield, tapping out a rhythm on the roof. It finally seemed like winter, the few feet of snow they'd gotten this week sinking them into the doldrums of January.

"I'm fine. Too bad we didn't have this weather a few weeks ago."

"Yeah, it feels more like the holidays now."

They quieted down again, both lost in their own thoughts and the Rihanna song now playing. She pushed on the gas even more, climbing the huge hill in front of them. They were heading up in elevation, and the snow certainly let them know it. She couldn't see anything in front of her.

"Maybe I should pull over," she said, her stomach plummeting with fear. Driving in this weather unnerved her.

"We're fine. Just keep going," he said, yawning as he spoke.

The ice intensified, larger chunks crashing into the metal truck, drowning out Rihanna's voice. Jessica told herself to breathe deeply, that it would be fine. Todd was here. They were in a big truck. Nothing else traveled on the road. They would be fine. She squeezed the wheel a little harder, giving the truck more gas as they climbed and climbed. She readjusted the hat on her head, a nervous habit, as she silently chanted a prayer to herself.

But the road suddenly got windy, and Jessica wasn't familiar with this stretch, wasn't expecting it, her foot heavy on the gas. Add to it the icy night, the already slick roads, and her nerves, and she was freaking out.

"Watch. Slow down, there's a huge curve," Todd shouted, alert now with fear.

Jessica did the one thing she knew she shouldn't. In hindsight, it was a disastrous choice, a choice her driver's education teacher in high school warned against. It was, inarguably, the worst choice to make. But she was tired, and when she was tired, she was irrational. She reacted. And that's what she did on the icy road.

She slammed on the brakes.

The sickening feeling of sliding out of control, the tumble down the incline, the scrape of metal, the screams coming from her own mouth—they broke the silence of the frosty, serene scene on the desolate stretch of road. She tumbled in the cab, tossed around like a feather in the truck for an eternity. Her stomach plummeted as she feared this was it. Her head felt like it was going to explode, tossed back against the headrest, the seat belt carving into her shoulder and chest. She couldn't breathe, the life force knocked out of her, her mind trying to process it all but the movement of the truck making it next to impossible. For a moment, as the truck continued to slide downward, skidding uncontrollably, she tried to turn to look at Todd, but she couldn't. For once, she couldn't feel the connection with her husband. She couldn't ask him for help or reassurance or to make it all okay.

Because it wasn't okay, she realized. This was nowhere near okay.

A sickening sound echoed in the cab as the truck pinged off

a solid object, the sound of crunching metal scraping against her brain.

And then everything around her went icy black.

Chapter Two

She tried opening her eyes, but darkness and confusion engulfed her. She blinked a few times, realizing her eyes were, in fact, open. She took in the sight, the silence, the hazy white glint of snow on the windshield.

"Todd," she croaked, reaching for him. Turning to him, her heart palpitating so fast she was convinced she was having a heart attack, she grabbed his hand and squeezed it. "Todd, are you okay?"

Her voice sounded like she hadn't spoken in months. It was scratchy and harsh, especially against the silence in the truck.

He squeezed her hand in response, turning to her in a disoriented haze. "Shit." His voice, too, sounded faraway, laced with confusion and fear. He winced, his fingers tightening around her hand like a vise. "My leg *fucking* hurts." Panic laced his words as he reached downward toward his leg.

For a moment, she sat motionless, not sure what to do, afraid to assess the damage but rationally knowing she needed to sort this all out. She couldn't ignore reality forever, couldn't pretend this hadn't happened. Her chest heaved, familiar worries creeping in. She shoved them down, knowing there would be time to deal with those painful memories later. She inhaled, loosening the seat belt against her now aching chest and shoulder. She pawed in her purse for her cell phone, pulling it out and lighting up the screen as a mock flashlight. She turned it, aiming it toward Todd's lower body to take a look at his leg, ignoring the pain in her shoulders and neck. Her heart stopped.

His door was caved in, probably from the ricocheting of the truck off whatever they'd hit. She panned the light down. His foot was twisted at a very bad angle. Even in her confusion and the darkness of the truck, the cell phone light made it obvious that something was terribly wrong. She didn't need a doctor to tell her the diagnosis.

"I think it's broken," she said.

"I don't know," he said, still wincing, his words a harsh chant. He pulled his pant leg up, his jaw clenched and face grimacing. Slowly, he peeled up the fabric. She panned the light lower, leaning to take a closer look. There weren't any bones poking through, which was a good thing. Still, it was banged up, twisted. He tried moving it, managing to move his ankle, but he gasped in pain. It already looked swollen. She took a breath, panning the light up so she could see his face, could meet his eyes with hers. Scrapes etched his cheeks, but they were nowhere near as bad as his leg. Todd's face and expletives said it all—this wasn't good.

"Are you okay?" His words pleaded with her, despite his still obvious pain. He breathed heavily, but he managed to look up at her, worried about her even in his state. His face contorted, his eyes squeezing shut as soon as he looked over at her.

Her hand went to her face, groping for a hidden injury. She felt fine, as fine as could be expected. She reassured Todd, "I'm fine. Just stiff."

She was physically fine, but mentally, she was a disaster. Her mind whirred with questions, with fear. They'd crashed. Todd's leg was hurt. She needed to find help.

She needed to help Todd, though, who writhed in apparent agony. One thing at a time, she reminded herself. One thing at a time.

She plunged her hand back in her purse, plucking out a bottle of pills.

"Here, take some of these for now," she said, handing him the tablets.

"What is it?"

"Ibuprofen."

"Great," he said, chucking a few in his mouth. "Does the label say for headaches and potentially broken bones?" He swallowed, passing the bottle back to her. She stuffed it in her purse. Maybe they would dull the pain. More importantly, they'd prevent him from getting a fever and help with inflammation.

She reminded herself to stay calm, to not freak out. They were tilted slightly forward, but she steadied herself on the dashboard.

Todd ran his hands through his hair, groaning. "Glad the

airbags work so well in this piece of shit," he announced.

"Yeah, really. And you make fun of my car." Todd always mercilessly teased her about her ten-year-old tiny hatchback he barely fit in. Still, he had little room to talk.

"All things considered, we're pretty lucky, I guess," Todd admitted, still breathing heavy from pain.

"If you say so," she said, not really feeling lucky right now at all.

"Okay. Let's assess the damage. My door's obviously not going anywhere. See if you can open yours," Todd ordered, and she obeyed. They needed to get serious, to figure this out.

"I've got it," she said, reaching for the handle in the darkness. Her eyes were adjusting, making it easier to maneuver. She tried opening the door. Nothing. She moved up against it. Still nothing. "Ow," she said as she twisted, her shoulder throbbing as she tried to contort to muscle it open.

"Okay, okay. Try the window," he said. Her window remained intact, the brunt of the damage to Todd's side of the truck. She rolled down the Chevy's old-fashioned windows, reeling the hand crank over and over, the window screeching, snow falling in on her. She stuck her head out the window, her phone lighting the path. She glanced around, squinting against the still falling snow. She didn't know what she'd been expecting to see or what she hoped to see.

She did, however, know what she saw wasn't ideal. Not even close.

"Shit," she said, still leaning out the window. "Shit, shit, shit. This is bad."

"What?"

"Hold on," she said, leaning out the window a little more. She was afraid she would fall out, but she balanced herself, her cell phone still serving as a flashlight. She gripped the phone so tightly, it hurt her hand.

After a minute of studying the scene, she crawled back in, rolled up the window, and exhaled.

"What is it?" For the first time since she'd realized Todd was alive, true, icy panic crept in. This obviously wasn't a good situation. Behind the exhaustion and the frustration, something else wound its way in between each and every snowflake slamming into the windshield.

Fear. Desperate fear.

"We're down an embankment, pretty far from the road from what I can judge. It's still snowing like crazy out there. We're in a snowdrift between a bunch of trees."

"Fuck." Todd slammed his head back, exhaling loudly.

"We're buried in the front here, and there are trees on either side. We're sort of wedged between them, so I don't think our doors will open." Jess tried to suffocate the fear swelling in her chest, focusing on the cold, hard facts. She tried to separate herself, to keep her mind objective. It was tough.

"Look again. See if you think we could get out and dig ourselves out."

"I don't want to fall."

"I'll hold on to your arm."

She sighed. "Todd, I know what I saw. I don't need to look again." She was frustrated, mostly at the situation, but her irritation increased with Todd too. "You never trust me."

"Hey, I trust you. But this is important. If we can get out

of here, dig out, we need to do it. Otherwise, we're going to be stranded."

The word "stranded" did it for her, put it into perspective. It had such a negative vibe to it. She immediately hoisted herself out the window again, the cold air and stray snowflakes slapping into her cheek.

She wormed her way farther out this time, hanging out as far as she could. Todd held on to her hand as she tried to study the situation more intently.

Her cheeks tingled with the biting snow and ice. She shielded her eyes, trying her best to look through the snowflakes, pulling her black hat down a little bit more. Visibility was awful, but a tree branch rested right above her head, close enough to touch. She turned to look over the top of the truck to assess Todd's side. With the door caved in, she figured things weren't promising. She was right. On his side, a huge tree strangled the truck. They were, in fact, wedged between two overbearing trees, sunk into a few feet of snow. They were being held hostage by lumber, and drowned by snow. The front end of the pickup was all but buried. With the embankment behind them, there was no way they could get the truck out, even if they spent the next two days shoveling. Of all places for her to go off the road.

Resigned to the bleakness of the situation, she gingerly inched back into the cab. "Um, yeah, it's just as bad as I thought. Todd, there's no way we're getting out of here, not from what I can see. Not with the angle we're in and the snowdrift. Even if we crawl out, we're in feet of snow. This truck isn't moving. It would never make it up the embankment.

It's impossible." The final word stalled on its way out, the realization of it slamming into her chest as she said it. It was impossible. It was hopeless.

They were done for.

"Fuck," he said again, slamming his fist against the door. He groaned as soon as he did it, the movement twisting his already hurt leg. He sucked in an audible breath. Several quiet moments went by in which Todd, laboriously breathing, apparently tried to assuage the throbbing pain and anger. After some time, he announced, "Okay then. We're going to need to call for help."

She nodded. They were going to be fine. A call to 911, a little bit of cold temps and discomfort until they could get to them, and they'd be okay. So they couldn't save themselves. It wouldn't be a quick fix, a simple back-on-the-road situation. It was fine. They'd get some help, they'd get out of here, and they'd be home. It would probably be closer to 6:00 a.m., but at least they had the day to recover. They'd have quite the medical bills, not to mention the lost truck. But it was okay. They were going to be okay.

She unlocked her phone screen to dial the number.

Then she saw it.

"Todd," she said, tears surfacing.

"Shit. We don't have service, do we?"

"Not at all. None. No bars."

"Let me see it," he said. She handed over her phone. He maneuvered it around the truck, trying not to jostle his leg.

"Here, try sticking it out your window," he said. She obeyed, rolling down her window again, trying to get a signal.

Nothing.

She slumped back into her seat, trying to think, trying to rationalize what they should do.

"We can't survive here for long," she said, saying what neither wanted to admit. She was already chilled to the bone, much of the heat in the cab having escaped during the window ordeal. She didn't want to think about how long it would be until the interior of the truck became lethal.

Todd responded by gently banging his head on his door. This wasn't the reaction she wanted. She panicked.

"What do we do?"

She looked at him, the man with the broken leg, hoping for the answer, the miraculous idea that would save them. She wanted him to fix this like he fixed so many things. He fixed everything in their house—the dishwasher, the deck, the drywall Henry chewed. Surely he could repair this. Logical, optimistic Todd would make this better, would get them out of this. This would just be some crazy story they told their coworkers on Monday, laughing about how messed up it had been. Todd would limp around in a cast, and his friends would sign it like high schoolers. He'd be mad because someone wrote something inappropriate on it, and they'd laugh about it over Chinese food because neither felt like cooking. He'd be off work for a while, lounging in the house playing video games and cooking his crazy concoctions. They'd take a picture and put it in their scrapbook, looking back at it from time to time, reflecting on the crazy, disastrous wedding they'd gone to that had ended in a snowbank. He'd make fun of her driving, and she'd blame him for his annoying singing and complaining.

They'd laugh and talk about how Todd's first real injury was a result of her driving, and then they'd move on and talk about the chicken tacos she'd made for dinner or the upcoming staff meeting or wing night at the pub.

"Well, we're not going anywhere if the truck's buried. I don't even think there's a hope of getting the doors open. Maybe we'll take another look when the snow stops or when it's light out." He slammed his head back against the headrest, eyes squeezed shut in frustration, pain, or both.

She took a deep breath to dull the disappointment simmering in her chest.

So that was his answer. Look again and pray they were wrong. It didn't sound like the miracle she'd hoped for. It didn't sound like much of a plan at all.

"It's still coming down hard," she observed, still not ready to resign themselves to a wait-and-see plan.

"And it's not supposed to stop, either. Shit."

Her heart started to palpitate again. "So *what* are we going to do?" Panic caused her voice to rise an octave. The prospect of sitting there, no plan in motion, was more agonizing than the fear usurping her.

He reached for her gloved hand, kissed it. "Calm down. We'll figure it out. Let me see if I have service by some miracle."

He grabbed his phone from his pocket, playing with it. It seemed pointless to Jessica. Still, she clung to the impossible hope. She had no choice.

Todd fiddled with his phone, responding with the answer she anticipated. "Dammit. Nothing."

"I know. We're in the middle of nowhere, remember?"

"Just our luck."

"We're screwed. No cars come this way. Plus, we're buried. It's freezing, and the snow's supposed to keep coming for days." Tears were flowing now, tears for Todd's leg, tears for the situation. Tears for the guilt. "We're *screwed,* Todd."

"Jess, calm down. It's going to be fine. We're safe right now. We're in the truck. We have over half a tank of gas. We're going to be okay. Someone will find us. We just need to stay here, sheltered from the storm. We can make it."

"It's Saturday at midnight. And your leg's broken."

"I don't think it's broken. I can move it some. I think it's just really badly sprained or something. Besides, someone will find us tomorrow. We just have to make it through tonight."

"So we're just going to sit here? That's it?"

"There's nothing else we can do right now. We just need to stay calm and be smart. We need to be patient. We're fine."

"I don't think we're fine. You're hurt. You need medical attention." Her chest burned with anxiety. She was already starting to feel claustrophobic, trapped in the cab of the truck, buried alive. She was cold. Her neck hurt. Most of all, she felt hopeless.

She took a deep breath, silence pervading the truck. *Think, Jessica, think.* They needed to get help.

She sighed, not liking the thought that came to her head. It was all they had, though.

"I'm going out there." Her voice, unwavering, steadied her own resolve.

"What? Like hell you are." He shook his head violently,

appalled at the announcement.

"Listen. We need to get help. Maybe if I wander up to the road, I can get cell service."

"Jess, we're in the middle of nowhere. There's no way."

"I can't just sit here. I have to try. If I can get my phone to work, we could be out of here in no time."

"I don't want you going."

"Well, genius, you went and hurt your leg. What, you think we can make you a makeshift crutch from a tree limb?"

He sighed, seeming to be lost in thought. Finally, after a long pause, he shook his head, as if in disbelief the words were actually going to come out of his mouth. "You go straight up the embankment and come right back. If you're not back in five minutes, I'm coming after you, bum leg or not."

"Deal." She realized she'd been wringing her hands, fear over what she was about to do threatening to take over. She didn't let it. She had a plan. She needed to see it through, needed to try to right the wrongs of the night. She needed to try to find them hope to hang on to.

"Here. Take my coat with you." He undid his coat, passing it to her. It was a laborious task, as he was still in agony over his leg. When he finally handed it to her, she graciously accepted it, just the thought of the whipping snow chilling her already cold body. She wrapped the coat around her shoulders, putting the hood up, and tucked her arms inside.

Todd groaned as he leaned down under the truck seat, grabbing something and holding it up between them. "Put these on too."

Squinting and grasping for the item, she realized he held

two boots. "Your welding boots? Ew."

"Now is not the time to worry about designer shoes. Put them on. They'll keep your feet warmer than those things you have on."

Shrugging, she obliged, twisting and turning to get her shoes off and putting the way-too-big boots on. She tied them as tightly as she could, her gloved hands making the task difficult.

"Jess, listen. On your way back, I need you to do something else. Make sure the tailpipe is clear of snow. Try to dig out around it. That way, we can use the heat in the truck without getting carbon monoxide poisoning."

"Got it." She leaned over to kiss him on the lips, closing the gap between them quickly, her mind set on the task at hand. "I'll be right back," she said.

"You better be."

With that, she rolled down the window again, feeling inspired by her latest take-charge initiative. She wasn't letting the snowstorm win. She would take care of things, like she always had. She'd gotten them into this mess; she was getting them out of it.

***

Trudging through the snow, her hair whipping around her face, she was glad she'd taken Todd's coat and boots, even if the boots were weighing her down. The wind stabbed into her cheeks. Visibility was so awful, she feared she'd never make it back to the truck.

"Keep it together," she said aloud, choking on some snow as she did, zipping Todd's coat up tighter and burying her face low inside it, the smell of Todd's woodsy cologne creeping up toward her, enveloping her in its familiar scent.

She stomped forward, cell phone in her pocket. This was a disastrous idea. Still, what choice did she have?

She plodded on, feeling like she'd walked ten miles, each footstep a chore. In reality, it had probably only been about ten feet, the whirring snow making it difficult to walk in a straight line. She tried to follow the tire tracks of the truck, swerving in the deep ruts in the snow. They'd slid a long way, she realized. They were fortunate they hadn't slammed into the trees head-on. Things could be much, much worse. They were actually quite lucky, even if it didn't feel like it.

She pushed forward, her lungs heaving in the icy cold air, burning from it. Her calves ached as she trudged up the embankment, thankful for her boot camp exercise class.

"Just keep going," she said, chanting to herself like a crazy person. When she couldn't go up another step, she pulled out the phone, saying a silent prayer. She squinted, turning sideways so the snow wasn't blowing right in her face.

The glow from her cell phone creepily illuminated the blackness of the wilderness. She unlocked the screen, searching for the bars.

Nothing.

"Dammit," she screamed, her voice ricocheting off the trees. She stomped in the snow like a toddler throwing a temper tantrum. Losing all hope, she dialed 911 anyway and waited to see if it would work.

Nothing. As she'd expected. Still, the searing reality of their predicament burned in her chest, in her mind. Her plan failed. There would be no miraculous solution to their predicament, no easy out.

She shoved the phone back in her pocket and attempted to toss her hair out of her face. She turned around and started making the depressing descent back to the truck, to Todd, to the desperate situation.

When she got to the truck, she remembered Todd's words despite her anger. She knelt down by the exhaust, using her gloved hands to scoop the snow off it, kicking it away. She worked for ten minutes, shoving snow away to create a decent clearing around the pipe. At least they'd have heat for a while. Cup half-full.

Or frozen, in this case.

She slumped back to her side of the truck, frozen to the bone, enraged at the core, fearful of what the rest of the night would bring.

***

After she hauled herself back through the window and dusted off the snow, Todd reached over to pull her in close, helping her peel off the wet outer coat, the damp gloves, the soaked boots. Exhaustion claimed her as its prisoner.

She changed back into her shoes and graciously accepted Todd's gloves. They spread the wet articles of clothing on the dash to dry out some. They were both already shivering.

When she settled back into the darkness, the despair finally flooded her system fully.

Tears poured down her face as she released her frustration, anger, and fear. Todd didn't ask about the phone, her sad state obviously telling him everything he needed to know.

"Hey, stop sobbing. If I'm going to be stuck in here with you all night, I do not want to listen to you bawling. I'm the one with the injury here, and I'm not crying."

"You have some tears," she said through her sobs, wiping at her eyes.

"No. It's allergies."

"Stop it, manly man. You have a right to cry."

"I'm not crying. Now listen, let's make the best of it, huh? Just like we always do. This is nothing," he assured, scooching over to her, groaning as he shifted his leg. He wrapped her in his arms and kissed her tear-streaked cheek. "We're fine. Stop being Miss Doom and Gloom."

"We're not fine. You know it."

"Shh, sit back. Calm down. Just breathe."

She wiped her tears away, blinking them back as best as she could. Todd's heart thudded against her back, his scraggly beard scratching her cheek. She felt for his face in the darkness. "I'm scared."

He didn't say anything, just kissed her neck, exhaling what were probably fears and worries of his own. They sat for a long minute, and she squeezed her eyes shut. For a luxurious moment, she let herself be transported away from the frigid truck, from the sorrow, from the intensity. She drifted away in

Todd's arms, the warmth of his body, the comfort of his love wrapping around her, calming her. She basked in the presence of him, let the strength of Todd's arms reassure her.

When her breathing had slowed and her tears had stopped, he kissed her cheek once more, snapping her back to reality. This was real life. Todd's arms, Todd's love couldn't make the situation any less dire. They needed to focus, to be smart. They needed to survive.

"Reach under your seat," Todd whispered in her ear, apparently sensing the moment was gone as well.

"Why?"

"There should still be a tarp there from when I helped Jeff last weekend with painting their house."

"Why do we need a tarp?"

"To cover the window," he said, shaking his head.

"Oh. Right." His window had cracked in the wreck. Luckily, it was still intact. Still, covering it would help insulate the truck, especially with cold air creeping in through the banged-up side.

She fumbled in the darkness, twisting and contorting to reach under the seat. Her hands felt the familiar plastic. She handed it to Todd.

Grimacing from the pain of his leg, he twisted to put the tarp across his dilapidated window. He reached under his seat and retrieved a roll of duct tape. He began making a crude window cover, Jessica watching, rubbing her hands on her arms.

"Good thing I'm a so-called redneck, huh? Nothing duct tape can't fix."

"Except your leg, maybe," she teased.

He settled back in, his work done. "Well, actually…," he said.

She laughed a little in spite of the situation.

With the first problem of many somewhat solved, at least for now, she settled into the situation. An unsettling silence filled the space between them. He leaned back over, pulling her into him again. His body warmth flooded through her chilled body.

And then he spoke.

"Do you remember when we first met?"

She rested against him, the tightness of her chest softening some more. She managed to smile, in spite of the pain in her neck and the butterflies in her stomach. It was her favorite story, her favorite moment.

"I know what you're doing," she said.

"So let me."

She nodded, letting him whisk her away from the freezing truck, the fear, and the peril. She let him pull her right back to where it all began.

Chapter Three

She'd been watching him from across the room all night... not because she was attracted to him, but because he was so damn out of place.

Polite conversations, hors d'oeuvres Jess couldn't pronounce, and champagne toasts filled the country club. She sat at a table of people she didn't know, answering polite questions about her schooling and career. She even muscled through questions about her family, the most awkward of all. She hated when people asked about her family, like that was who she was. At a table of polite and proper strangers, though, she gracefully nibbled on the odd, fancy foods and laughed at the right moments. It was a beautiful, elegant wedding.

But misery tainted her perspective. She felt out of place, bored, and out of her comfort zone. This was not her scene.

She took another sip of her champagne, wondering how

long until she could politely escape from this event of the century. She fluffed her black ball gown, which still made her feel underdressed. She'd bought it on a bargain website. Around her, all the women were asking each other who they were wearing. She prayed they didn't ask her, or she'd have to say she wore Formal for Less instead of an actual couture designer.

Business execs and people who were important and people who thought they were important filled the dance floor. Shoulder to shoulder, they were tangoing, foxtrotting, and other forms of boring dance she couldn't pronounce or understand in their probably overpriced designer shoes. Raising her glass to her lips to eradicate the nervous tension she hadn't quite shaken off, she stared across the room at the only other person who looked completely out of place—him.

While all the men in the room wore tuxes, bow ties, and other variants of formal attire, he did not. He wore faded jeans, a tucked-in button-down sans tie, and sneakers. He had a full beard, which, to be fair, was neatly kept. Still, he was far from the clean-shaven, tux-wearing men all around.

Jess noticed a lot of people were staring at him. She found her eyes wandering to him repeatedly too. She was curious about who the heck he was and how he got on the invite list.

Victoria made her way with her new husband to Jess's table.

"Jessica! I'm so glad you made it. It's been so long. Anthony, this is one of my good friends from college, Jessica. She's a schoolteacher now. Thank you for coming."

Jessica leaped out of her chair, as was expected, and

gave Victoria the traditional "you look beautiful" and "great wedding" compliments. She painted on the overdone smile to convince her old friend she was having a blast.

"It's so good to have my PSU days represented. All the other girls were out of town or busy," Victoria said, still clutching Jess as they hugged, her scratchy veil irritating Jess's arm. She smiled through, though, truly glad to see her old friend, if not truly comfortable at the event.

She was glad she'd come to support Victoria, the sweet girl from a different chapter of her life. She enjoyed seeing her old roommate happy and living the life she'd dreamed. Still, if she'd known she would be the only one from the college crew coming, she probably would've stayed home. She could be on the sofa right now, cuddled up with a book or watching some cheesy chick flick, tossing back some beer and popcorn. But that was the risk of not staying in touch, she supposed. You ended up at places like this... alone.

She made more small talk before the glowing bride and groom made their way to another table. Jessica decided that while she was up, she may as well go to the bar and get more champagne. Her stomach rumbled audibly. She knew it was probably a bad idea to drink so much on an empty stomach, but her boredom and discomfort made it seem like a viable option. It was a wedding—it was okay to hit up the alcohol a little more than usual, right?

They'd already had "dinner." At weddings Jessica had been to, dinner meant fried chicken or ham or steak or barbecue ribs. It meant hearty and filling. Wasn't that supposed to be the best part of a wedding, after all?

Apparently, Victoria's family thought dinner meant a single piece of shrimp and some fancy vegetable appetizers she couldn't pronounce, along with some cucumber sandwiches. She couldn't wait to get some real food on the way home. Her mouth watered at the thought of a huge burger and fries with a milkshake on the side.

After ordering another champagne at the bar, she grabbed a handful of peanuts, hoping they would at least sustain her another hour or so until she could make an exit. The band started playing a slow song, and Victoria and Anthony made their way to the center of the dance floor for their first dance— foxtrot style, of course.

"So, are you dying for some real food, too?" a husky voice whispered in her ear. She almost choked on a nut, the deep voice sending chills down her spine. She turned to see who'd spoken to her.

It was him. Jeans man.

He looked rugged, backwoodsy, if she had to put a word to it. He was bulky—not fat, but not a twig, either. She couldn't help but notice his biceps seemed ready to bust out of his button-up, in a good way. Up close, she noticed some tattoos on the top of his hand. She suspected he had more.

He wasn't her type, not really. Not that she necessarily had a type, and, if she did, her type these days was nonexistent. She hadn't been one to date. She'd seen enough screwed-up family situations to know a man wasn't the answer to happiness, not in her mind.

Still, on the rare occasion she let her mind wander, let herself consider the possibility of falling in love, the man before her was not the one she imagined herself with. She had a thing for tattoos, true. But she'd always pictured herself with a clean-shaven man, a bit of a nerdily dressed man. The man before her was not him, not even close.

Looking at him, though, his eyes lit up from within, and she felt something foreign. A simple flutter, a feeling pulsing through her veins. She couldn't quite identify it. In fact, she chalked it up to the champagne she'd just downed. Standing there before the man in the jeans with the tattoos and beard, though, she knew there was something. There was something that made her want to answer him, to talk to him, to linger near him a little longer.

Gaze locked on him, she noticed something else too. Those eyes. God, those eyes were perfect. They shimmered and taunted her, telling her he wasn't quite an angel, but he wasn't a devil, either.

She smiled, leaning in to whisper, "I'm starving."

"Me, too," he said, slapping his stomach for effect.

"Bride or groom?" she asked, holding her champagne glass.

"Bride. Cousin of the bride. Distant cousin. Like the distant cousin they usually keep in the closet, distant."

Jess blushed. "Oh, I see."

He scrunched his nose, slapping his head. "Oh, not like that kind of closet. Definitely not that kind of closet."

She laughed. "Well, okay then. Not that it matters, either way."

"Of course it matters. I don't want some gorgeous girl like you thinking I'm in that *closet."*

She shook her head, not really knowing how to answer that. She took a sip of champagne.

"How about you?"

He had a hand in his pocket, further accentuating his cool, casual vibe. He wasn't intimidated by the setting, by the dress code, or perhaps even by her. Not that he should be intimidated by her, she reminded herself. They were just talking about the wedding. He, like her, was just feeling trapped by boredom. There was nothing more there.

"Um, no closet for me, either," she said, grinning.

"I meant bride or groom."

"Bride. We went to college together."

"Really? What for?"

"I was an education major."

"Are you a teacher, then?"

She nodded. "High school English."

"So you're a book nerd."

"I'm not a nerd," she retorted.

He raised an eyebrow.

"Okay, okay. A little nerdy."

"There are worse things." He smiled, his free hand stroking his beard in an oddly charming gesture.

"I suppose." She twirled the stem of her champagne glass, eyes still locked on his, then dragged her gaze away to watch the rest of the newlyweds' endlessly long first dance, not really sure why she was still talking to jeans man other than the fact that he was there. It was nice to talk to someone else who was out of place and not afraid to admit it.

"So, what's your name, book nerd?" he asked, interrupting

her thoughts.

"Jessica. You?"

"Todd."

"Nice to meet you, officially."

They stood, taking in the elaborate dance between Victoria and Anthony as the wedding guests politely looked on.

Todd leaned in, whispering in her ear. His breath caressed her neck, sending chills down her spine again. Her cheeks warmed. She needed to slow down on the champagne.

"So, I have a proposition," he said.

She took a step back. "Um, yeah, no."

"Easy, cowgirl. Not that kind of proposition."

She eyed him suspiciously.

"Seriously. Not that you're not gorgeous or that I wouldn't like to proposition you in that way. But look at me. I love food. I love to eat. And right now, my knees are shaking from the freaking seaweed they served us and claimed was dinner."

She laughed at his accurate depiction.

"So how about we sneak out, ditch this formal, stuffy affair, and go get some real food? There's an amazing twenty-four-hour diner down the street. They've got the best mac and cheese."

"The best? Really?"

"Listen, you might not know me well, and you might not really trust m, but when a chubby guy tells you it's the best mac and cheese, you listen. I don't have many areas of expertise, but food is one of my fortes." He patted his stomach again. It was odd. It was sort of charming too. He wasn't too into himself. She couldn't help but smile.

She looked at the wedding, at the cake that needed to be cut, at the fancy event in front of her. A good friend would say "no, thanks" and suffer through the rest of the event. She should be polite, deal with her growling stomach. A responsible adult wouldn't go sashaying off into the evening with a man wearing jeans to get some mac and cheese. It was ludicrous.

But, in all honesty, Victoria wasn't a close friend anymore. This was the first she'd seen her in the two years since they'd graduated. She was tired of being here, tired of doing the right thing all the time. For the first time in a long time, she felt the need to rebel, to do something a little crazy. She felt like doing what she wanted when she wanted, for no other reason than because she wanted to do it.

Like go get mac and cheese with this odd man wearing jeans whom she didn't even know.

Maybe that was just an excuse for her to ditch this uncomfortable event that was so out of her league. Maybe it was an excuse because she was starving and wanted nothing more than mac and cheese right then.

Or maybe it was because, for the first time, a guy managed to make her want to say "yes," even if it was just to an impromptu trip to a nearby diner.

So she did. She took Todd's arm, slinked out the back of the country club, and headed to the mac and cheese, some laughs, and the date that would seal her future.

***

"You were so beautiful in that black dress."

"It was a bargain dress."

"Still looked the best out of all those women."

"And you looked…."

"Homeless?" Todd teased, his breath still warming her neck. The temperature continued to drop, but she felt relaxed and safe now. He'd calmed her, like he was so good at doing.

"Sort of. But you were still sexy."

"What did it for you? The sneakers? The belly pat?"

"You were so suave."

"I know. I get that all the time. I actually had to beat a few women off me before we got to talking that night."

"Really?" She grinned, shaking her head.

"Really. But I'll tell you another thing. That was the best freaking mac and cheese."

"Well, yeah. You assured me it was."

"Yeah, but I was just hoping."

She leaned back to look at him. She could tell his eyes were twinkling, even in the dark.

"You said you always got their mac and cheese." She shook her head, not quite sure what he meant.

"I lied."

"What?" She was flabbergasted. They'd told this story time and time again. They'd always talked about their mac and cheese date.

"Truth. I never ate at that diner before. I'd just seen it on the way in."

"How dare you lie to me," she said, slapping him playfully. She shook her head.

He shrugged, laughing. "I had to get you to trust me somehow. Figured it seemed less creepy if I said I'd been there before."

"You are a creep. I can't believe you've been lying all this time."

"A man can't reveal all of his glorious secrets. Plus, it worked, didn't it? It got you to give me the time of day. And it was damn good mac and cheese."

She sighed. "I don't even know you. When we get out of here, I'm divorcing you for starting our marriage on false pretenses."

"Okay. Please, take me to court over mac and cheese."

"I will."

He nuzzled her with his nose. "You won't. You love me too much."

She just groaned. "Damn mac and cheese liar."

"A guy's gotta do what he's gotta do. I had to impress you somehow."

"Did I look like the type of girl who would be impressed by mac and cheese expertise?"

He quieted for a moment before responding. "You looked like the kind of girl who would make my life fun and awesome and complete."

"Well, obviously."

"So humble, you are."

"Why are you telling me this now?"

"Well, I figure you can't be too mad since I have a hurt leg and all. Plus, I'm your only company and entertainment for who knows how long. You can't stay too pissed at me."

"Are the pills working?" she asked, changing the subject. His leg still didn't look good, and from the expression on his face when he moved, it wasn't feeling too good, either.

"Yeah, they're working. They're taking it from 'fucking kill me' pain to 'fucking kill me in a little while' pain."

"What can I do?"

"Nothing."

They snuggled into each other, her head on his chest. For a moment, she pretended they were at home on their couch, snuggling in for a nap after dinner like they sometimes did. She pretended they were under her favorite red-checked throw, the lull of the boring news in the background as she relaxed into him, the warmth of his body and the nearby fireplace easing her into a state of peace.

Before she could sink too deeply into the fantasy, though, reality settled in. They weren't at home. They were nowhere near it.

The guy and the girl from the mac and cheese date were lost, blanketed by snow in the middle of nowhere. And she didn't know if they would ever be found.

Chapter Four

"I should've listened to you," she said a few moments later, the truck chilling noticeably. She trembled, rubbing her hands on her arms in a sad attempt to warm up.

"Of course you should've. Haven't you learned I'm always right?"

"Ha. Not even close."

"Come on, when am I wrong?"

"All the time."

"Give me one time."

"Um, when you thought we should just put one more twenty in the slot machine at Rockygap Casino last week. You had such a 'lucky feeling.'" Despite the darkness of the cab, she used air quotes on the last words for emphasis.

"That doesn't count." He dismissed her with the wave of a hand.

"We lost. And then we lost another twenty after that.

And another."

"Okay, okay. One time I was wrong."

"Or how about when you said you found the best deejay in the entire world for our wedding?"

"So he lost power in the middle. No one noticed."

"He lost power for an hour. We had to hum the bridal dance song. When people talk about our wedding, they always bring it up."

"Please, it was no big deal. It was fun. People remember our wedding because of it. Plus, it could've been worse. At least we had real food at our wedding. Doesn't count. Try again."

"Or the time you thought we should put a 200-watt bulb in the lamp to make it brighter and almost burned the house down. Or when you said my bid on the house was too low, or when you thought you saw Keith Urban in Pittsburgh at the diner or—"

"Okay, okay. I get it. I'm wrong sometimes. But just sometimes."

"You were wrong when you said we're fine," she murmured, getting serious.

"We are. Look at us, walking down memory lane. I'm thankful we're stuck here. What a story we'll have someday." He nudged her with his arm, but she wasn't in the mood for his jesting.

"Stop it, Todd. It's not all a joke, you know."

He quieted at her snippiness, and she felt bad for bringing down the mood. They let the silence wrap them up, creep between them. She tried to calm herself, to remind herself it would be okay. She just hated feeling so trapped, so helpless. She needed to do something.

"I'm going to stick my scarf out the window," she said, feeling like she needed to do something.

"You should save your scarf to stay warm." The statement had logic, she had to admit. Still, practical wasn't her strong suit, not in this situation.

"It's red. Maybe someone will see it if they're driving by." She could hear the desperation in her own voice, but she refused to acknowledge it. So it was a long shot. They still needed to try something.

"They're not going to see it."

"And yet another time you're going to be wrong."

He groaned. She unwrapped her red scarf from her neck, wound down the window, and tied the scarf to the rearview mirror. Snow fell on her lap, shocking her. She watched the other end of the scarf flutter out the window like a beacon in the ocean of snow before she reached down to roll the window back up, stifling the influx of cold snow.

"Leave the window cracked," he said.

"No way. I'm freezing."

"Exactly. Leave it cracked. Let's see if we can get the truck to start for a few, get some heat in here."

"Then why would I leave the window cracked, genius?"

"Carbon monoxide poisoning, genius."

"I cleared the pipe already, remember?"

"That was a while ago. Plus, this is you we're talking about."

"What's that supposed to mean?"

"Need I remind you of the time you put motor oil in the wrong place in your car? I'm a little concerned whether you actually cleared the exhaust pipe."

She scowled. "That was one time. I know what a damn exhaust pipe is."

"I'd rather not take our chances. Better safe than sorry."

"Pretty sure this isn't safe. At least if we got carbon monoxide poisoning, we might be warm."

She wouldn't admit it, but she knew Todd was right. She wasn't exactly handy. She was probably the worst person you could ask to be stranded with in a survival situation. Bear Grylls would murder her in five minutes. Good thing Todd was smart about survival. Good thing he loved her.

She could explain the difference between a participle and a gerund. She knew Shakespeare's birthdate and Poe's first story and what a dangling modifier was. But hands-on survival? These were not her strong suits. Sure, she'd survived some impossible situations in the past, had shown her mental strength. She'd survived the most gut-wrenching loss of her existence and had learned to move on after Bailey. She'd somehow managed to find a way to not think about her every second of every day, to find a sense of joy in life once more. Todd always told her she was a survivor in every sense of the word—but she was the first to admit that surviving in the wilderness or doing anything mechanical was completely out of her league. Thank God she hadn't been stranded alone, or she'd probably be dead by now from some silly mistake.

Todd had always been the opposite. Give him hands-on living, give him experience, give him something to fix. He was a welder, but he was good at just about anything he could do with his hands. Cars, electrical, household repairs—he was a man's man when it came to fixing stuff.

Just don't give him a test, a book to read, or anything academic.

They balanced each other in that way and in so many more. She saved money, always afraid of what might be coming down the path. He spent money, encouraging her to splurge on a new haircut, designer jeans, or a new chair for the house. He tried to convince her to go to Fiji when she tried to sell him a staycation. She hated cooking; he loved it. She liked being active, being on the go. He loved kicking back and relaxing. She was a cat kind of person; he preferred dogs. She followed the rules, for the most part, at least as an adult. He broke the rules. They swirled in contradictions. They were a walking dichotomy.

But they worked. They worked from the moment they met because they were also the same in so many ways. They were outliers in so many social circles, the ones on the fringes by choice. They liked people, sure, but their quirks put them outside the normal social rings. They were easily amused and a little bit wild. They both had a free spirit within them, a wild child wannabe soul that only strengthened when they were together. They made each other want to explore, to be adventurous, to live it up. They brought out the rebels in each other, the life livers, the fun chasers.

Together, they were a functioning but crazy couple, living in the adult world of responsibility but straying from the normal every now and then to experience life to the fullest.

Together, they could get through anything. She had to cling to that.

She perked up at the thought of having some temporary relief from the cold as Todd wriggled to get closer to the driver seat, being careful to not jiggle his leg too much. He reached over to the keys, turning it with a whispered "Please."

Nothing happened.

"Shit." He slammed the dashboard in frustration. His temper was always one of his flaws.

"Let me try," she uttered, reaching for the key in his hand.

"It's not working."

"Move."

She shoved him away, trying the key herself, whispering "Please." If her toes weren't so damn cold, she'd cross them all in hopes of the engine coming to life.

She turned the key and laughed at her luck. The engine chugged to life.

"Wrong again," she gloated, a huge grin on her face.

"You know, I should push you out in the snow."

The smile stifled itself at his words, even as the sound of the engine underscored her hope, emphasized the soon-to-be warmth that would be theirs.

She didn't respond to his statement, lost in her own bout of regrets and guilt.

"Jess?" he asked finally, concern in his voice.

She warmed her hands in front of the heater. It already felt heavenly, even though it wasn't even close to being completely warm. Finally, she responded in a disconsolate voice, "Probably should. This is my fault."

"Hey, stop it. Don't blame yourself." He put a hand on her arm, shaking her a bit.

"If I'd listened…."

"We might still have ended up here, or worse. Things could be worse. We could've hit a tree head-on. By some luck, we landed right between them. It's all okay. It's all going to work out." He, too, rubbed his hands in front of the heater.

"I love you," she whispered, still feeling guilty, still not quite believing him. This was her fault. She'd messed up, big-time. Who knew what price they'd pay for it.

"I love you too."

She smiled again, leaning against him as she basked in the warmth of the heat radiating through her fingers. They sat, wordless, reveling in the simple but heavenly feeling.

Todd interrupted the silence a few moments later. "You do know, when we get out of this, I'm never letting you live this down."

She groaned, shaking her head as she pulled away from him. "You just said it's not my fault."

"Of course I did. Because right now, I can't blame you or I look like a dick. Later, though, oh man, is this going to be a great addition to my amateur comedic stand-up at parties."

She rolled her eyes, elbowing him in the ribs. He was quite the comedy act at all of their family and friends' functions. She'd always told him he should've tried his luck as a comedian instead of a welder. She hated to admit it, but he was pretty funny, even if it was usually at her expense.

After a few minutes, he turned the engine off, and her morale instantly plummeted again.

"Oh man," she whined. For a few minutes, she'd forgotten how shitty things were. It was funny how a few minutes of warmth could do that.

"We've got to be careful. Ration. Speaking of which, let's see what treasures we can find." He started in the glove box, clicking it open and plucking out some loose papers. He dug to the bottom, finally pulling out a Snickers.

"Score. One Snickers. Oh, and here's a pack of M&Ms," he said, shaking the treasures in front of her.

"So that's where those went," she shrieked, hitting his arm. "Those were mine."

"Well, I bet now you're glad I stole them, huh?" He placed them carefully on the dashboard. "We need to try to save them for tomorrow."

"Did you put one of those survival kits in here like I told you to back in August?"

She'd watched a segment on *Dateline* about survival. It had given her a list of survival items. She'd put a box in her car and told Todd to put one in his, paranoia creeping up on her. Flighty Todd, though, had waved his hand in the air. He'd said something like, "Real men don't need survival kits. They just need their bare hands." She'd commanded him to just put it in his truck anyway. As usual, he'd shucked it off as another item on the expanding to-do list, the one that never seemed to get done.

"Um, no, didn't get to it."

She grimaced. "Just your two hands, huh?"

"Shut up. I had no way of knowing."

"Which is exactly why you should've put it in here. I have

one in my car."

"Which would've been really helpful… except your car is out of commission, isn't it?"

She grimaced again. He always got the last word.

She'd sort of forgotten to change the oil in it. For nine months. Now the engine was kind of destroyed.

Okay. Completely destroyed. As in not even drivable in the slightest. He did have a point. Still, she wouldn't admit that, of course.

"Not my fault. You're the man. You're supposed to be on top of these things."

"If you say so. Anyway, let's keep looking. Reach under your seat. I think there are a few sodas under there."

She leaned down, reaching around again, and found two Mountain Dews stashed way in the back. "I thought you gave up soda?"

"Again, thankfully not."

"But the doctor said—"

"Well, I like my Mountain Dew. And again, it's a good thing I'm a rebel."

"I suppose. Except for the snow emergency kit. That probably would've come in handy."

Todd rustled under his seat and managed to pull out a hoodie, which was dirty but warm, and a blanket. There were also three half-empty bottles of water.

"There we go. Who needs a fancy survival kit? Look at this. Score."

He passed her the hoodie before tucking the blanket around them.

"You keep it," she said, handing back the hoodie.

"Stop. Put it on. You're smaller than me. Less internal heating power."

She had given him back his coat already and had to admit the one she had, although stylish, wasn't really very warm. Next time she bought a coat, she'd perhaps be analyzing its warmth instead of its pattern. She sighed, taking the grease-smelling hoodie and putting it on. She was thankful for it.

They settled in, momentarily relieved by their treasures. She handed him another dose of ibuprofen.

"How many do we have left?"

"Um, almost a whole bottle."

He popped them into his mouth, swallowing them dry. They needed to find help soon. An infection could eventually set in, and over-the-counter anti-inflammatory medicine wasn't going to cut it. They had no way of knowing just how bad it was, although the swelling didn't look promising. It could actually be broken for all they knew. If they didn't get it fixed soon, who knew how bad things could get. Jess knew complications could arise from the smallest injury. Coupled with the cold, it wasn't a good situation. She shrugged these thoughts off, trying not to let her mind race down the ugly tunnel of what-ifs. She couldn't go there, not now.

"Poor Henry's going to be so scared," she said, her mind wandering again, but not to any happier thoughts. At the thought of him, her heart panged.

"He'll be okay. I left the light on for him, and he had plenty of food when we left."

"He's never been home alone all night."

"He'll sleep right through. We'll probably be back before he even wakes up."

"I hope so," she said, tearing up at the thought of him waiting for them. She'd give anything right now to kiss his nose or to rub his floppy ears.

"You know, I distinctly remember a time when you threatened to divorce me over that dog."

She scrunched her nose. "I don't remember."

"Yes, you do."

"Nope. I always wanted him."

"Liar. You hated him."

"Yeah, I guess I did." She grinned, thinking of how stupid she'd been.

"You did. Do you remember when you wouldn't even speak to me because of him?"

She sighed, her mind traveling right with him to a time in the not-so-distant past, a time when she'd just about had it with Todd, with their marriage, and most of all, with the dog named Henry.

***

She was making salsa chicken in the Crock-Pot when Todd came home from work, grinning ear to ear despite the summer heat. On a day like today, Todd was usually miserable when he finished his day of welding, a day of sweating behind his torch. Today, though, she detected a bounce in his step and a smile on his face despite the ninety-degree heat.

"What are you so happy about?" she asked as she paused

from stirring the chicken to look at him.

"Coming home to my gorgeous wife." His words lilted like a melodic song, his steps jaunty. Something was definitely up with him.

She eyed him suspiciously, resuming her stirring. "Okay, what is it? The lottery? A new woman?"

He kissed her on the cheek. "Even better."

She turned, full attention on him. He pulled out his phone to show her an e-mail.

Congratulations, Mr. Kling. We are contacting you because you are next on the waiting list for a brindle mastiff puppy. Due to someone backing out, he is now yours. He will be ready for pickup August 22. Please forward the initial deposit to reserve him.

"I don't understand," she said, handing the phone back to him after reading the cryptic message.

"We're getting a puppy. A mastiff, just like we talked about."

Jessica froze. "What?"

"Remember, we talked about this last month? About putting our name on the waiting list?"

"Yeah, but you said it was a year wait."

"It is. But we got lucky. They have one for us. Isn't that great? This never happens, from what I hear. Most people wait at least a year. We got so lucky."

Jess just stared at him, unable to process his words.

"You're not smiling. Why aren't you smiling?" He set his lunch box down on the counter as he studied her.

"Because we agreed we wouldn't get a dog until next year." Her voice remained calm and collected, but there was definitely tension rising within. She breathed deeply, trying to

remain rational.

"I know, but this is crazy. No one gets a puppy in a month. We can't turn him down."

"Yes, we can. I start teaching that week. And I'm teaching at a new school with new kids. I'm going to be busy. I have lesson plans, new books to read, and a million after-school activities to run. I don't have time to be worrying about training a puppy right now. Plus, you're working all the time, especially with all of the overtime coming up. You'll barely be home to help out, and I don't have time for this right now, Todd. I didn't even want a puppy to begin with, but I agreed we could get one in a year or so. This is too much." She stated her case firmly, her eyes drilling into his.

His face was soft, boy-like as he pleaded with her. He was like a child begging Santa Claus for the bicycle he just had to have. "But it'll be okay. I'll help. Mac says they're so laid-back, not like a regular puppy. You'll barely notice he's here."

"No, we can't. Sorry, but no." Her anger surged, the prospect of Todd being so insensitive to her stress bugging her. How could he possibly think this was okay? How could he even consider this as a good idea? He knew the stress she was dealing with after switching jobs. How could he even suggest this?

She exhaled, prepared to spew more reasons why they couldn't possibly buy a puppy right then. Turning, though, she saw his face. His dejected face, his sad eyes. Probably sensing he was getting to her, he even put out his lip in his best rendition of a pouty face.

Jess found it disturbing, not endearing.

"Please. You'll love him. Plus, I'll do absolutely everything," Todd said, approaching her, wrapping his arms around her as she stood by the Crock-Pot.

"I said no." She made sure her voice sounded as icy as she felt.

Todd exhaled. "Fine then." He'd stomped off like a four-year-old. Jess felt bad for a millisecond, but then she breathed a sigh of relief. She'd talked some sense into him. This was a terrible idea. They'd just moved into a new house, and she was starting her new job. They didn't have time for this. Cats were one thing, but a slobbery, peeing dog was something else completely. She had nothing against dogs overall—she just didn't want to deal with one right then.

She finished making dinner as she smiled. She'd dodged a bullet. That was that. Todd would be sad for a few days, but he'd forget all about it. They'd go on with their standard routine, with their perfect little world. She'd acclimate to her new job, sans puppy, and everything would be fine.

They didn't talk about the puppy anymore that night, or even in the next few weeks. Todd seemed to take the decision really well. Jess was even surprised that he'd accepted defeat so easily. Still, she didn't question it.

Looking back, she should've known something was going on. For stubborn Todd to give up without a fight was unheard of. She should've seen the signs.

She didn't, though, not until it was way too late.

Two weeks later after the "no puppy, no way in hell" conversation, Todd did something he never did.

He defied her wishes. He ignored her pleas.

He brought home the floppy, twenty-four-pound mastiff and set him before her.

She cried and threatened to divorce him. They fought, the puppy peed on the floor, and she vowed never, ever to even give the vile beast the time of day. She spent the next month hating the puppy and scowling at Todd every now and again. She didn't mistreat the puppy. She fed him. She took him out to pee. She neutrally accepted him as much as she could manage. She just made sure everyone knew she wasn't happy about it, especially Todd.

She told herself she loathed him. She hated the way he chewed on her pant leg when she tried to work on lesson plans. She hated the way he ate her favorite shoe or peed on her new Vera Bradley tote. She hated his cries at two in the morning every morning. She hated how she'd just get comfy on the couch and he'd start bawling. She hated his incessant barking, his crazy antics, and his whining.

She just plain hated him. She felt like she'd hate him forever.

But somewhere in the first month, somewhere between her periods of rage, something else crept in, something unexpected. It snuck into the picture like a thief in the night, possessing her without her even realizing it was happening.

Between her anger and her frustration, something Jess never expected crept in for the brindle mastiff puppy they named Henry. It was so unexpected, she couldn't even pinpoint exactly when it happened, when the crossover occurred. She just woke up one day months later and realized she didn't feel hatred for the puppy or regret. She didn't feel frustration, anger, or annoyance.

She felt only one thing for the puppy she hadn't wanted from the beginning.

Love.

Love in its purest, truest form.

***

"And now he's the best thing that happened to us. That's me, being right again." Todd nudged her as if to underscore his point.

"I suppose I'll give that one to you. He is pretty awesome." She smiled, thinking of the now full-grown mastiff at home on their couch. She'd been true to her word those first few weeks. She'd ignored him when he tugged on her pant leg. She'd yelled for Todd across the house when the puppy had to pee or when it chewed up a can of soda or when it chewed up the table leg. She'd ignored his soft brown eyes or his whimpers for her attention.

But when, out of the blue, she realized she loved him, everything changed. She was buying him toys and looking forward to patting him on the head when she got home. That dog had won her over with his huge paws and big heart. Now she was obsessed with him. He was her best friend, and she had turned into one of those crazy twentysomethings who treated their dogs like a child. Henry's social schedule rivaled her own most weeks, and she always rushed home to maximize her time with him.

"See why you should always listen to me?" Todd said,

interrupting her thoughts.

"Let's not get crazy here."

"You just can't admit when I'm right."

Jess sat back and closed her eyes, the cold seeping in. She hoped he was right this time. She hoped she would be listening to him gloat in the coming years about how they were fine after all. She hoped against all the odds that she'd be at their next party listening to her family roar with laughter about Todd's jokes about this situation, Henry cuddled up to her side comforting her. She hoped she'd spend countless nights on the couch, her mastiff companion drooling on her sweatpants as he begged for a bite of her cupcake. She'd give anything right now to be sitting with the big, floppy dog who had once been a puppy she'd hated.

She'd give anything to go back to those nights when the worst thing that happened to her was a puppy crying and interrupting her sleep or peeing on the floor. She'd give anything to go back, to shake the woman who stewed over the prospect of a puppy, and tell her there were worse things in life.

Chapter Five

"Jess, wake up. Come on."

Jess opened her eyes, confused at first. The blackness swarmed around her again. Her cheeks were tight with cold.

"How long did I sleep?"

"Probably a half hour or so."

"Why'd you wake me?" She stretched her body, her neck still achy from the wreck and her legs stiff from sitting in the same position.

"We need to move around."

She raised an eyebrow in the darkness, despite the futility of the movement. "Oh yeah?"

"Yeah. We need to at least move our fingers and toes around. We don't want frostbite setting in."

"I thought a perk of being snowed in would at least be no exercise class."

"How do you think I feel?" He gestured toward his leg,

which was probably throbbing like crazy.

Jess leaned away from him, moving her toes and fingers around. They were tingling, prickly from the cold.

"You know," he said suddenly, "if you'd rather, I can think of other exercise forms to warm us up."

"Really? You have at least a sprained ankle, we're snowed in and practically dying, and you're thinking about sex?"

"A guy always has to try."

"You're ridiculous." She laughed, readjusting her dress again and fluffing her wavy hair in spite of the circumstances.

"Okay, let's start the truck for a moment or two again. We've got to warm up somehow, and since you're being so difficult...."

She shook her head, still moving her fingers and toes. Todd leaned over, crying in pain when he twisted his leg.

"Let me do it, hero," she said, pushing his hand away and reaching for the key. She twisted it in the ignition.

The truck sputtered.

"Shit." She tried again. It revved and crackled, but wouldn't cough to life. She tried again and again, not wanting to give up. "Dammit!" she screamed when her attempts proved futile.

"Hey, calm down. Breathe."

She nodded. They had to get the truck started, though. If they wanted to survive, they needed to get it working.

She tried again, crossing the fingers on her other gloved hand.

Finally, after what felt like forever, it hummed to life. She leaned back against the seat, relief flooding her. Todd gripped her arm in a congratulatory gesture, patting it before letting go.

They soaked in the heat of the truck, the wind whipping around outside. For a moment, they could ignore the howling and blowing, the tree branches slapping the windshield. They could forget about the snow piling on the truck, the hopelessness. They could focus on the heat, the warmth caressing their cheeks, bringing color and life back into them.

When they shut the truck off, painfully, all willpower focused on the task, they sat in silence, the lashing wind the only sound. Despair overpowered them every time they shut off the truck. It was a reminder, a slap in the face—a cold one—that things were desperate. With the end of the blasting heat came the end of their sense of normalcy, the end of their ability to feign optimism. When the heat stopped and the iciness slowly eked its way back in, its gnarled fingers grappling with their psyche, any false hopes dissipated. They returned to their forlorn state of realism, of truth, and of cold.

"We need to insulate our heads. All of our body heat escapes from there," Todd declared, getting down to business as soon as the heat stopped.

"I've got a hat and a hood."

He raised an eyebrow. "That hat doesn't really look like it's doing much."

"It's stylish."

"My point exactly. It's not exactly made for the arctic tundra."

"Sorry. I forgot my knitting needles. How the hell do you suppose we make hats?" she teased. She was, however, thankful for the distraction, thankful for something to focus on.

"Improvise," he said, looking around the truck. He ran his hand over the truck seat. "The insulation in the seat will be perfect."

He pulled a pocketknife from his pants, groaning from the twisting he had to do.

"Will you sit still? You need to stop moving your leg."

"Here," he said, panting from the effort. He handed her the knife. She grimaced.

"What am I supposed to do?"

"Cut a piece of the fabric from the seat near your window. Then cut some of the insulation out too. We'll cut it thin enough to tuck inside our hats, give us extra insulation."

"That's actually smart."

"Hey, just because I'm no book genius doesn't mean I don't know things."

"Truth. I'd have never thought of this."

She carefully opened the knife, her eyes adjusted to the darkness. She meticulously turned in her seat, eyeing the fabric, gingerly digging the knife in. She didn't need to hack her hand off on top of all their predicaments. Slowly, with full concentration on the task, she dug the blade along the seam of the fabric, cutting out a crude square. She touched the foam inside the seat, also cutting a small, thin square out. When she'd accomplished the job, she cut the foam piece down the middle, sawing away at it carefully, being sure to avoid cutting herself. She took her time, creating a sad excuse for a hat. It certainly wouldn't win any awards in fashion.

She handed a square of insulation to Todd, who took off his hood and winter hat. He put the thin square on top of his head before maneuvering his hat on top of it. It was hard, awkward work, but he eventually wriggled his hat overtop the piece of insulation.

"A little bulky and not so attractive, but it will do." He put his hood back up.

She began doing the same, bending the thin piece of foam around her head, tucking her hat and hood around it to keep it in place. It was bulky, uncomfortable, and awkward. But if it could help her keep any warmer at all, she'd do it.

She tucked the knife away, setting it on the dashboard. She settled back into Todd, tired from her impromptu fashion designing. Tim Gunn would certainly not be proud in any way of her attempt.

They sat in their bulky headwear, melancholy settling over the truck, the gloom of the situation kicking into full gear. They were stranded in the snow, no hope of being found, survival becoming a serious thought in both their minds. What had started as a joyous trip to a friend's wedding and a good time had left them here—cold, hungry, in the darkness.

At least they weren't alone.

At least they had each other.

They could get through, she encouraged herself. They could get through together.

This time, she decided it was her turn to lift the spirits.

"Do you remember last summer, when we went to the zoo on a whim?"

She leaned against his cheek, his beard tickling her face. His cheek muscles moved in a smile.

"I remember your barbecue hot dog." He laughed, a belly

laugh now, rocking her entire body.

"Shut up. Of course you'd remember that."

But she laughed, too, thinking about a time when a barbecue-sauce-covered hot dog was the biggest worry.

***

Things were not quite going as romantically as they hoped. Of course, they were in a zoo in the ninety-four-degree heat.

It'd been an admirable idea, a romantic surprise on Todd's part.

A trip to the zoo. Not exactly the passionate experience of most twentysomethings' dreams. For Jess and Todd, however, it was perfect.

He'd refused to tell her where they were going, insisting she got in the car that Saturday morning and not ask questions— which was hard for her. She was, in all admission, a bit of a control freak.

Nonetheless, she'd obliged, with him promising it'd be worth it.

When they'd pulled up to the Hershey Park Zoo, her grin widened.

"You remembered." She turned to him, the huge smile still plastered on her face. Her heart swelled with happiness.

"Yeah, of course I do. It's been five years."

"Five years since you told me you loved me in front of the jellyfish tank." She laughed.

"You say that like it's a bad thing."

"Not a bad thing. Just different." She winked at him, and

he shook his head.

Pulling his sunglasses away from his eyes to look at her, he smirked. "What's wrong with different?"

"Nothing at all. I just sort of know why your family keeps you in the closet," she teased, and he tickled her.

"Will you ever let that go?" he asked over her squeals of laughter. She finally pulled away, slapping his hands in the process.

"Nope," she responded, breathless.

"Get out of my truck, you unappreciative jerk."

"Wow. Last time we were here, you told me you loved me. Now that we're married, you bring me here to call me a jerk?"

"Yep. That was the plan."

"Well, I like it."

They walked into the zoo hand in hand, just like they'd done the last time. She smiled at the nostalgic feeling.

They'd metaphorically walked through so much since the last time they'd sauntered through the zoo entrance. A wedding, moving, a dog, fights, and dreams. They'd lived through burned spaghetti dinners and random date nights and family visits from hell and friendships lost. Here they were, though, five years after their first "road trip" date, the first time he'd admitted he loved her, still hand in hand. She smiled at the cheesiness of it, but at the sweetness too.

It fit her, the girl who only wore mismatched socks and who everyone teased for quoting Edgar Allan Poe in high school. The girl who ate pickles on every kind of sandwich, even meatball; the girl who liked to dance in the rain on a whim. The somewhat nerdy, quirky girl fell in love with a man who wore jeans to weddings and confessed his love in front of highly disliked sea creatures.

And now that man belonged to her. They headed toward the front entrance to buy their tickets, still hand in hand. He held the front door open for her once they reached it and gestured for her to pass first.

"After you, ma'am," he said, and she slapped him for calling her ma'am. He knew she hated that.

The zoo attendant working the cash register looked at them, either for the slap or for the fact that two twentysomethings were coming to Hershey, not for the park but for the zoo. Alone. Without children.

They paid for their tickets and walked through the zoo, still holding hands just like the first time. The exuberance of the zoo brought out the child within her. Jess ran to the toucan exhibit, one of her favorites, and snapped pictures on her phone. They made a smashed penny and took a selfie by the bear exhibit. They dashed through the exhibits, looking at all of the creatures, racing to locate the elusive creatures in the cages before each other. They read out random facts from the plaques and oohed and awed over every animal.

Everything was going well... until they got to the exhibit.

The jellyfish tank.

They walked, strangely misty-eyed, Todd ready to give his heartfelt speech about love and marriage and her.

But a sign hung in front of the glass....

We're sorry, but this exhibit is temporarily shut down as we prepare to move the jellyfish to a larger exhibit.

The glass aquarium was empty, other than the cardboard sign. The jellyfish were gone.

Jess's face fell into a mock frown. Todd looked sort of angry.

"Really?" he said, hands in the air.

She shook her head, smirking.

"What?" he asked, looking at her.

"Nothing. It's just sort of funny."

"What is?"

"How angry you are over jellyfish. People are probably starting to worry."

"Well, I just wanted it to be special. I wanted to recreate the moment. But without the jellyfish here, it's just not the same."

She giggled freely, leaning on the wall beside the exhibit. "Only us."

He laughed too. "Only us." He leaned in, kissing her passionately by the empty exhibit. "Jellyfish or not, I love you."

"I love you too. But can I ask you something?"

"What?" He pulled back to look at her.

"Why'd you pick the jellyfish to confess your love?"

He shrugged. "It was cool in here. There was air conditioning, and it just seemed like a good moment."

"Okay. Just curious." She scrunched her nose at him, and he returned the gesture, smiling.

"You know, it shouldn't matter if we were by a dumpster. I told you I loved you. That's all that matters."

"Yeah, it was special. But jellyfish? At least you could've

picked something super cute like the naked mole rats."

"The naked mole rats? Who the hell finds naked mole rats cute?"

"Um, excuse me. Do you even know me?" She pretended to be horrified, but Todd just rolled his eyes. She laughed again in spite of her act.

"You're impossible." He wrapped his arm around her waist, pulling her in closer.

"Pretty much." She leaned into him, resting her head on his shoulder like she'd done so many times before.

"Can I ask you something?"

"You will anyway, I'm sure," she teased.

"If I'd have confessed my love in front of the naked mole rats, would you have said it back?"

She paused, seriousness taking over. She looked into his eyes, feeling a little bit of regret. "No. I just wasn't ready, you know? I'm sorry."

"Don't be sorry. It all worked out."

"You were probably devastated." She thought back to that moment. His words that day had rocked her. She was falling for him, but she couldn't bring herself to say them back. She wanted to say those three words she'd been guarding her whole life. She wanted that moment in front of the jellyfish to be their big moment. Fear took over, though.

"I was a little disappointed, in truth. But I knew you would come around. I saw it in your eyes. I knew you just needed time."

"I did love you in that moment. I did. I was just afraid." She squeezed his hand as they walked toward the exit of the building.

"I know."

She smiled at him, remembering the moment from years ago. "You were so patient with me."

"I'm amazing. Clearly."

She nudged him, but inwardly she agreed. He hadn't let her know he was disappointed when she couldn't return his words. He hadn't pressured her when she said she needed more time. He'd just smiled that day, kissed her cheek, and pulled her to the next exhibit. They'd had a beautiful day together, confessions of love or not.

And in truth, she'd spent the day reveling in the fact that he loved her. That day, he'd torn down one of the bricks in her carefully constructed wall. He'd helped her see possibility. It was a turning point in their relationship, one they could appreciate now as the true step toward their forever.

They wandered back outside, the sun scorching them. "Whose idea was it to come to the zoo when it's this damn hot?"

She squeezed his hand, perspiration making their hand-holding a little more gross than romantic at that point. "I'm starving. Let's go get some food."

He agreed, and they headed to the food area to order lunch. Going with their streak of bad luck, if you could call it that, the food stand had run out of chicken tender baskets, so they'd had to get the hot dog and fries basket.

"Romantic," she teased, and he shrugged.

"What's wrong with hot dogs?"

"Nothing, I suppose."

She took her tray over to the condiments, slathering her

hot dog with relish, of course, and ketchup, her go-tos.

"What smells weird?" she asked, looking at Todd. He threw his hands up. "No, not like that, weirdo. I mean, it smells like… barbecue sauce?"

She looked down at her hot dog, then looked at the pump in front of her.

Todd started laughing immediately. "You put barbecue sauce on your hot dog."

"No, I didn't. It's ketchup," she argued, confused.

"Yes, you did. Look." Todd, already snickering, pointed toward the pump she'd just used.

Jess read the sign. Sure thing. Although the condiment pump was red, it most certainly did not read "ketchup."

It said barbecue. She'd just put barbecue sauce all over her hot dog. With relish.

"Oh God, gross! No way." She made a Mr. Yuck sticker face, trying to wipe off the barbecue sauce with a napkin.

Todd wheezed with laughter.

"Shut up."

"Do you want me to go get you a new one?" he asked.

Her pride kicked in.

"No. I like it like this."

"A barbecue sauce wiener? Yum. Sounds great." He chuckled some more.

She flipped her ponytail before marching to the seating area. She claimed a seat under an umbrella, Todd following.

She bit into the hot dog and almost gagged. Barbecue and relish. Not a good mix. And on top of it… the hot dog was cold.

Todd kept laughing the whole lunch at her face of disgust.

"It's not so bad," she said, trying to convince herself.

"Yeah, okay." He rolled his eyes, still grinning at her predicament.

She eventually gave in and laughed at her own stupidity, at the day, at the weirdness of them.

After she'd choked down lunch, they'd finished wandering around the zoo. She felt warm, her cheeks and shoulders tight.

"Babe, you're getting burned," he observed as they strolled by the eagle exhibit.

"No, I'm not. I put on sunscreen this morning."

"Which one?" he asked, stopping on the path to the bear exhibit to look at her.

"Why?"

"Well, the one tube expired last year. I shoved it on the bathroom sink."

"What?" she snapped.

"Yeah, it was old." He shrugged.

"So why did you put it on the sink? Why didn't you throw it out?" Her voice rose. What the hell was he thinking?

"I don't know. I forgot."

"You idiot. I used that one this morning. Todd, really? Why the hell would you put it back?"

Todd grimaced, shrugging. "Oops. Maybe we should get going?"

She exhaled, exasperated, but didn't say a word.

"Maybe it won't be too bad. We were indoors a good bit," he offered, trying to salvage the date. She nodded, hoping he was right and that the tightness in her cheeks wasn't related to sunburn.

But that night, when she screamed in pain from the shower, when blisters covered her shoulders from the severe burn, she could only glare.

And Todd could only shrug and say, "At least you got to try a barbecue hot dog, right?"

***

Despite the pain and the cold, Todd chuckled even now, thinking about the story.

"Ew, I can still taste that hot dog," Jess said, shuddering from the cold and the nasty memory.

"Your face was everything." He laughed again, and she grinned in spite of herself.

"Well, despite the stupid hot dog and the sunburn, the trip was a sweet gesture."

"That's not what you were saying that night."

"Yeah, I know. But it was sweet. The whole meaning behind it."

"Wonder if other couples celebrate the anniversary of their first 'I love you.'"

"Wonder if other couples celebrate it at a zoo with jellyfish and hot dogs." She shook her head, the craziness of it, of them, getting to her.

"I wouldn't have it any other way," he said, serious now.

"Same here. You're a weirdo. But I love you."

"Yeah, well you're not so normal yourself."

It was true. They were a bunch of oddballs, laughing at stories no one else would think were funny, going on dates to places their friends wouldn't be caught dead at. They still ate Lunchables for dinner, still made a pitcher of grape Kool-Aid every week. They went to the movies to see animated films and went mini-golfing every week in the summer. Their idea of date night usually involved going to Burger King instead of a fancy, mature restaurant. They were two adults but still children at heart, still looking for fun in every moment.

Not that their life was a constant string of excitement. They had their dull moments, their moments dictated by routine. Overall, though, they were a little screwy, a little simple in their lifestyle.

And she loved it. She loved how she fell in love with a formal-attire-hating, jellyfish-confession kind of man.

Barbecue sauce hot dogs, sunburn, and all.

Chapter Six

Jessica tried not to think about the minutes slowly, painstakingly ticking by. Usually, the nights felt short, the warmth of her bed calling to her to stay longer. Most nights, she just put her head on the pillow, and the alarm blared a second later. She and Todd, neither fond of mornings, would groan simultaneously, rolling over after one of them hit Snooze.

Tonight, the night felt like an eternal disease, an unwelcome visitor. It overstayed its welcome, for sure. It dragged its feet, tiptoeing by at an angering pace.

It wouldn't quit. An annoying alarm would be a welcome reprieve, a celebrated victory. How quickly things could change.

Todd, pale and a bit sweaty, sat in silence, the pain of his leg wearing on him. She popped open the bottle of ibuprofen and handed him more medicine, hoping to at least dull the throbbing in his leg.

"We need to do something about your leg," she said after he swallowed the pills.

"Know any good doctors around?"

"No. But I have watched a lot of episodes of *House* and *Grey's Anatomy.*"

"Call me crazy, but I feel like that doesn't qualify you."

"Well, not like there are many choices around here," she said, brushing hair out of his eyes. "I think we should at least try to make a splint or something to keep it straight and still. We don't know if it's broken at all, and a splint will at least up your chances of it healing correctly."

"Oh, sure. Hold on, let me just grab the splint-making kit from my truck."

"Well, we need to be creative, just like the hats. Listen, I might not be a survivalist, but at least we can try."

"I mean, yeah, it's just my leg." He elbowed her, letting her know he was teasing. Deep down, he was probably terrified, though. She knew she was.

She tapped her chin, considering what they had to work with.

Then she remembered the tree branch.

"What if we fashion something from a tree branch?" She shrugged, thinking it was an okay idea for the circumstance they were in.

"What are we, going all primitive here?"

"If we have to. There's a branch on top of the truck. If I can break some smaller branches off, we might be able to use your duct tape or some of the seat belts to hold them in place, keep your leg straight. It's not going to be perfect, or hell, even good.

But it's a start."

He sighed. "I don't want you going back in the cold."

"Well, you've got to do what you've got to do, right? Stay put."

She leaned over and rolled down the window again, the air slapping against her so hard, it took her breath away. She steadied herself, inwardly chanting a "you can do this" mantra. She flung herself up on the window, the awkward dance now familiar to her, and dangled her feet inside the cab. She held on to the sides of the window, steadying herself so she didn't fall, Todd leaning over to hold her thighs. Snow blew into her face, fell on her coat, down onto her legs, but she fought against the cold. She felt around for the branch, pulling it down closer, gritting her teeth from the effort.

Some smaller branches extended from the main one. They weren't super sturdy, but they would have to do. She tried snapping them, but they were too big and her hands were too cold.

"Pass me your knife," she shouted back inside the truck, her hair whipping in her face.

"Jess, you're going to hurt yourself. No." He shook her legs, trying to coax her back inside. She didn't budge.

"Just pass me the damn knife, or I'm going to have to haul this entire snow-covered branch down."

He sighed, reluctantly handing her the pocketknife. She carefully steadied herself on the window ledge again, opening the knife, sawing at a branch close to her.

Her hands, her cheeks were getting colder and colder. Her face numbed, and she could barely see what she was doing.

She was, in all probability, going to hurt herself. Then she'd have to hear Todd's "I told you so." Still, she worked away, sawing with the tiny knife until she finally cut through the branch enough to snap it off the rest of the way. Delicately holding the knife in one hand, she carefully fed the snowy branch to Todd through the open window. She gouged herself with some wayward twigs on the way, and she worried she would poke Todd's eye out. She managed, however, to get the dilapidated tree through the window without doing any more damage to anyone or anything. She focused her attention back on the branch, working on cutting a second branch that appeared to be about the same thickness.

When she'd successfully cut through it, she folded the knife up, handed it back in, and pulled the second branch in with her.

She rolled up the window, dusting some snow off herself.

She took a few deep breaths, tired again from the exertion. Despite her exhaustion, it had felt good to be able to do something instead of just sitting, waiting for things to get better.

Removing her gloves, she spread them out on the dash to dry again.

"Okay, Bear Grylls, now what?" Todd attempted to dust some of the snow off the branch, his gloved hand tossing chunks of it onto the floor.

"Now we work on the splint." She eyed the two branches as best she could in the darkness. They were close to the same length, one a bit longer. She opened the knife, hacking at the end of it so it was the same length as the other. She crawled toward Todd's lap, the branches making the maneuver difficult.

"Whoa, easy now. I'm not complaining, but I don't think this is the place, you know?" He laughed, and despite the situation, she hit him.

"Shut up. Now straighten your leg. We need to try to set it so the sprain or whatever it is doesn't get worse."

"What's that mean?"

"It means it's going to hurt like a bitch. But we've got to try to straighten it. It's bent weird. Here, hold my phone." She turned the flashlight on and had him aim it down toward his leg. She took a deep breath, chanted her mantra again, and leaned down.

"One…," she started counting, putting her hands on either side of his leg.

"Wait, what?"

"Two…," she continued. She had no clue if this would work, but she had to try.

"Jess, you don't even—"

"Three…," she screamed, interrupting. She pushed and pulled with her hands, trying to straighten the leg. Todd shrieked in agony, a guttural sound that made her cringe in empathy.

She felt something pop and looked down. It still wasn't right. She hadn't been strong enough to put it back. In fact, she probably had made it worse, her luck. It hadn't really been a great plan in hindsight. Still, the angle didn't look quite as funky.

"Jesus Christ, woman. I think you're trying to kill me."

"I would've done that a long time ago," she said, reaching

for the branches. "Hold this in place." She put one branch on one side of his leg, and Todd, still groaning, reached down to hold it.

She lined the other up on the other side of his leg, reaching for the duct tape on the dash. She tightly taped the branches in place, pulling on the tape as hard as she could. She worked her way down his leg, aiming to keep it as straight as possible.

When she'd gone through the entire roll, his leg taped up with the branches holding it straight, she eyed her work.

It wasn't perfect. Hell, it didn't look good at all. She doubted it was even doing anything.

Nonetheless, it was something. At least she'd tried to do something

"All done." She brushed her hands together, getting the remnants of the branch and snow off her hands as best she could. She inched her way back to the seat, admiring her work in the dim glow of the cell phone flashlight. It wasn't much to look at, truly.

"Good as new. I think I can go for a hike now," he teased, gently patting his thigh.

"Better than nothing, I guess."

"Maybe."

She leaned back, exhausted from the cold and her efforts. Todd leaned in, kissing her cheek. "You know, you're one sexy doctor."

"Oh, I know. Clearly. Especially with this hat," she joked.

She looked into his eyes. She was still terrified, still sick to her stomach about their predicament. Looking at Todd, though, hearing him laugh with her, the fear disintegrated.

Even here, in the middle of nowhere, the scariness of their situation not far from her mind, he could do that for her. He could make her smile, make her feel safe.

"You know, there's no one I'd rather be trapped with," she said, nuzzling against his neck.

"Thanks, I think. Although next time, how about we get stranded on a hot tropical island? Preferably one with a real doctor. And some margaritas. I would kill for a margarita."

"Alcohol and pain meds? You're a rebel."

"You know it."

He pulled her in and held her tight, just the way he had for so many years.

Chapter Seven

"Let's have a few M&Ms and a sip of soda," Todd said, and Jess quickly agreed. She knew they needed to be smart, to be careful. But she was starving.

They each took a few M&Ms and a few sips of the soda they'd thawed in front of the heat the last time they'd turned on the truck. There were only a few drinkable sips.

"How long until someone starts looking for us?" Jess asked quietly, afraid to hear the answer but needing to talk about reality for a moment.

Todd took another sip of soda before responding. "Well, my mom usually calls Sunday night," he practically whispered.

That was so long from now. Even if she realized right away something was wrong and didn't just chalk it up to bad cell phone service, it would be a long time before rescue crews would be dispatched. Then there was the whole dilemma of if they'd even find them and how long it would take. Could they hang on that long? How could they possibly hang on?

She shrugged the thought off, deciding to get out her phone and check for service again. Maybe by some miracle....

But there was no miracle. Not this time.

"Maybe someone will see us from the road. Once the skies clear, once it's light out, they might be able to see my tailgate." His voice lilted, a fake optimism driving his words.

Jess knew it was ridiculous as she heard the sentences float in the cab. She had to hope, though. She had to believe. It was tough, however. Reality quickly floated to the surface. "Yeah," Jess said noncommittally, knowing it wasn't true.

She had to shove the pessimism out of her head, though, or she'd snap. It scared her to think of the truth, of the reality. She snuggled into Todd, his arms grasping her tightly.

He reached up and took off his beanie, placing it on her head.

"What are you doing?"

"You're so cold. Take it."

"But...."

"No buts. I'm bigger. For once, my lack of dieting motivation is a good thing. I've got more body-heat-producing capabilities than you. See, don't you wish you'd eaten more burgers instead of salads?"

She adjusted the hat on her hair, not worrying about hat hair in the slightest. She didn't respond to his joke, didn't smile. Instead, she did something a bit rash.

She abruptly stretched out her fingers, leaning to her left, and honked the horn. The blaring noise scared Todd. He actually jumped a little.

"Jesus, Jess." He clutched his chest for effect.

She laughed in spite of herself. "Hey, it might help."

"Huh. Yeah, that's a good idea. We should probably hit it every thirty minutes or so, just in case. But we have to be careful or it will drain the battery."

"See, I'm not so stupid."

"Never said you were. Me, on the other hand...." He shrugged as if in defeat.

"I've never called you stupid," Jess replied.

"Really? You can't think of a single time?" Todd elbowed her. Jess's face melted into a soft grin of admission.

"Okay. I've never called you stupid a single time since we've gotten married."

"Oh, right. Just our wedding day. In front of all the wedding guests."

"To be fair, there were only fifty people there."

"Oh, only."

She grinned as she rocked herself, trying to stay warm. It was becoming harder with each passing minute. The temperature dropped by the hour, the wind picking up even more. Even with the heat from the truck at random intervals, she shivered, her fingers aching from the lack of blood flow.

"Well, to be fair, I *was* kind of stupid."

"I'll say."

They leaned into each other, floating to a time not too different than tonight, a time of freezing cold temperatures, of truck problems, and of life-changing events.

***

Her hands were trembling, the single poinsettia shaking as she turned to look at Kim. "Where is he?"

"It's fine. He'll be here soon." Kim put a hand on Jess's shoulder, trying to offer comfort. It wasn't working.

Jess peered out from the back of the church. The pews were sparse due to a small invite list. Unlike most weddings, the groom's side had more people than hers. A few of the foster families from the years had come, and one friend from high school. She wasn't sad about it, though. It was just part of her life. When you moved homes every few months, friends were hard to come by.

She was sad, however, at the prospect of being a jilted bride.

The priest walked to the back of the church.

"Jessica, any idea where Todd is?" he asked, his voice soft and comforting. He clutched his Bible tightly, his fingers tapping out a nervous rhythm on the cover.

Kim took the lead. "We've tried to call him, but he isn't answering. I'm sure he's just running late. He'll be here."

Kim steadied Jess, who was still shaking. The priest nodded, heading to the front of the church, still tapping on the cover of the holy book. The guests were also getting antsy, checking their watches, their eyes fluttering around, their murmurs audible.

"He'll be here. I know he will," Kim said. It didn't reassure Jess that much.

Kim didn't even know Todd, didn't really know Jess very well. She was a work friend, a fellow English teacher she'd known for less than a year. They'd gone for a few drinks, had lunch together sixth period. They were work friends, but certainly not best friends. Jess had been embarrassed to ask her to be maid of honor, but she didn't really have a choice.

She didn't have any best friends to lean on.

Now, though, she was thankful for Kim, thankful for a friendly voice comforting her. Because in her heart, she didn't feel reassured. She felt like a fool, all of the certainties about their love taunting her now, teasing her.

She'd been an idiot to think someone could love her like this. Certainly, their love was real. But now Todd was realizing what a major step this was, how he just couldn't do it. He couldn't commit. It was just Jess's luck. She'd finally found someone she could lean on, could trust. She'd found someone who promised he wouldn't make a quick exit, stage left, like everyone else who was supposed to be there for her.

Yet here she was. Alone. All alone, waiting for another person to show up when they were supposed to, waiting for the unconditional devotion she'd yet to experience. Waiting to believe humans were worthy of trust, that relationships were possible.

Another agonizing half hour went by, and the tears started to form. Jess stared at her ballet flats, her knee-length dress now feeling foolish, scratchy, and uncomfortable. Her stomach lurched over and over at the thought of what this all meant, of how it was over before it had officially begun. She should've never let him in, should've never let her guard down. She knew better than to trust. Love had blinded her, though, like it did to so many. Love had made her believe in fantasy. Now the *fantasy imploded, her heart ricocheting off the leveled walls of the love she thought she could believe in.*

"Just give him a few more minutes," Kim pleaded, gently touching Jess's shoulder. Jess could tell Kim felt awkward, but she couldn't blame her. This wasn't typically part of the maid of honor protocol, especially when you barely knew the bride.

"Nope. I'm done." Her eyes were fixed on the pew in front of her, her teeth gritted. She'd made up her mind. She wouldn't do this anymore, wouldn't stand with their piteous eyes glancing at her. She'd been the pitied girl too many times. She was stronger than this. Tossing the poinsettia to the ground, she swiped at the tears, clenched her jaw, and did what she had to do.

She stomped to the front of the church, tears replaced with rage.

The guests and priest looked as she climbed the altar steps, her head held as high as she could muster. She turned to face the crowd, fifty grim gazes studying her every movement.

"I'm sorry, ladies and gentleman. Looks like there won't be a wedding. The stupid ass stood me up."

It was simple, frank, and honest. The crowd's eyes widened, as did the priest's—probably because of her word choice.

She didn't care.

Todd's parents rushed toward her, trying to comfort her. She brushed by them, stomping down the altar, her tears flowing freely again, her brave façade hastily crumbling as the shrinking, saddened woman came back.

She'd trusted him. She'd trusted in them. She'd finally trusted enough to give her heart over... and now, like the *poinsettia crushed on the floor in the back of the church, her heart tore apart.*

Just as she got to the back of the church amidst confusion and murmurs, another commotion erupted up front.

"Wait! I'm here. Here I am."

Jess turned to see Todd racing through the side door by the altar, his best man in tow. Sweat beaded on his forehead, on his face. His tie sat askew and there appeared to be dirt and scuffs on his pants. Stress painted his red face.

He looked like a wreck, not like a groom ready to pledge his life to the woman of his dreams.

The crowd, who had started to migrate from their seats, stood perfectly still, waiting to see what scene would unfold.

Jess didn't move, Todd rushing down the aisle toward her.

"Baby, you look beautiful." His eyes took her in, every inch of her. This, however, was not the scene she'd played in her head. This was not her moment to drink in his gaze on her.

He was here. He was calling her "baby," calling her "beautiful." She didn't feel any bride-like feelings, however. She didn't feel like calling him "baby."

She scowled in outrage.

"Yeah, real beautiful being stood up," she growled, hand on hip, not caring that fifty guests were still listening, frozen in place.

"That's not what happened." He gestured, stoicism on his face.

"Really? It's an hour past the wedding start time. An hour. You made me look like an idiot, you stupid ass. What the hell happened?"

Todd crouched to catch his breath. "I'm sorry. I had to run here."

"What?"

"I ran. From halfway from my house."

That was at least three miles.

"Why?" She shook her head, not quite following the story.

"We were on our way, Joe and me. I got a flat tire. We tried to fix it, but I didn't have a spare."

"So why didn't you call someone?"

"We both left our cell phones at home."

"Are you kidding me?" This just added to her rage even more.

"No. I wish. We waited for help, but we were on a back road. No one passed us. I knew the wedding was starting, so I decided a little broken-down truck and some snow wasn't stopping me."

"So, you ran here? In the snow?"

"Why's that so hard to believe?"

She smirked, the anger melting despite the circumstances. Todd patted his stomach.

"I'm kidding. I know. I think I might have a heart attack. So, what do you say? You want to get married?" He stretched a hand out toward her. She studied it, her arms crossed over her chest.

She pondered over his words. The beading sweat, the scuffed tux, the exhaustion and frustration on his face. It seemed like he was telling the truth. And if he was telling the truth, well, he was still a stupid ass... but she could forgive him for being a stupid ass who ran three miles in the snow to get to her, couldn't she?

"Aren't you freezing?" she asked, still trying to process everything.

"Um, no, not really. A three-mile run kind of gets the blood flowing."

She turned, noticing Joe, also wheezing at the altar. She turned her attention back to Todd.

"I thought you stood me up," she solemnly declared, staring into his eyes.

"Why would I do that?"

"I don't know." Her words were a whisper as she shrugged.

"I might not be the smartest guy, but I'm not that much of a stupid ass, believe it or not." He said it loud enough for the congregation to hear, and a few of the guests chuckled.

"Well, you're still a little bit of a stupid ass."

The priest coughed, and Jess mouthed, "Sorry."

"So, what do you say? You want to do this?" Todd asked, reaching for her hand again.

"I guess," she said, smirking. She let him take her hand and reveled in the feel of his skin against hers, in the trust being reclaimed between them. Todd gave her hand a squeeze. She squeezed back.

"You guess? I run all those miles, and you just guess?"

She kissed him then, a passionate kiss, and he wrapped his free arm around her waist.

"Can we just skip everything else?" he whispered to her. The priest, studying the scene, coughed again.

"We're ready now, Father. Sorry for the holdup," Todd said, raising his hand at the priest in a little wave.

"Places, everyone?" Kim asked, still standing nearby, the somewhat crumpled poinsettia in her hand. She carried it to Jess, but she waved it off.

"Nah. Let's just jump right in," Jess said, walking down the aisle with Todd as the organist rushed to play a rendition of "The Bridal Chorus." The guests, still bewildered, settled in, looking a bit fearful as well. Joe took his place at the altar, and Kim followed behind them, carrying her bouquet and the crinkled poinsettia.

It was an untraditional traditional wedding ceremony, but it was magical all the same. They'd learned early on that love wasn't easy. Sometimes it meant you acted like a stupid ass. Sometimes it meant you messed up. Sometimes it was equivalent to running a marathon in what was practically a blizzard.

But it was okay. Because at the end of it, they had each other, and that was all Jess could've ever asked for.

Chapter Eight

Sluggishly, the darkness caved to the light. The glimmer of day poured through, a weak flicker. A sliver of relief accompanied it. The icy blackness of the first night faded as the hours passed. They'd survived the night. They'd made it, their memories keeping them company and abating the lonely chill of the night's terrors.

Jess stretched, fatigue draining her. They'd managed to snag a bit of sleep here and there, usually after they'd warmed the truck for a few minutes. She rubbed her neck, still stiff from the crash and the less-than-cozy sleeping conditions. The truck's bench seats arguably made the situation a little bit more bearable, but it still wasn't quite their mattress in their warm, inviting bed. She rolled her shoulders, trying to loosen up her creaking bones, her aching muscles.

Yawning, she shook Todd awake. "It's morning. We made it through the night."

She passed him some more pills, glancing in the bottle. With this time schedule, he had enough to make it a few more days. Not that they'd need them, she reminded herself. They were getting out of here today. They'd survived the night, just like Todd said they needed to do.

She rolled down her window as Todd yawned and stretched. She sobered to see snow still coming down. It had definitely lightened up but still fell steadily enough to be depressing. The sky was gray, another storm hanging in the air. She sighed, slamming a fist against the window ledge.

"Still snowing."

"What did you expect?" Todd asked.

"A miracle."

"You have to make your own miracles," he answered pragmatically, and she rolled her eyes.

"We aren't having this argument. We need to get out of here."

"Agreed. I'm starving. Waffles sound amazing right now."

"Well, we need to get out of here first. So think. What should we do?"

"Why don't we try getting the truck out? It looks like our best shot right now," Todd said.

She shook her head. "There's no way. We're buried."

Todd pulled his fingers, cracking the joints. "What if we dig out?"

"You're hurt."

"Yeah. But we need to get out of here. It's going to hurt a lot worse if hypothermia sets in."

She shuddered at the thought of being stuck another day, another night. Todd was right. They needed to get out of here.

"We should try now before the next bad storm comes through," he observed.

"Agreed."

"We need to try and clear the tires, clear a path for the back end at least. If we can get some traction, we might be able to get the thing out of here."

"*We* can't do anything. Your leg." She pointed at it, as if he'd forgotten his leg was practically immovable.

"I'm not sitting here while you do all the work," he argued, shaking his head.

"So you're going to risk hurting yourself worse? No way."

"You can't dig it out yourself."

"Give me some credit. I've got this." She twirled a loose strand of hair sticking out from under the cap. She didn't know if she really "had it," to be honest. Still, her independent woman streak kicked in. Rise-to-the-challenge Jess made her want to go out there, kick ass, and get this truck on the road. She'd show him. She could dig them out, save them. She could.

"Jess, come on."

"You come on. If you go out there, you're going to mess your leg up even worse, so stop. I've got this. I'm tougher than you think." She added a wink at the end to reassure him. Still, thinking about the real prospect of digging in the snow for hours caused her confidence, her she-woman strength, to fade, just a little. Not that she'd admit it.

He looked at her. "I know," he admitted, softly, abandoning the fight.

She leaned in to kiss him, and he put his hand on her face, lingering in the kiss longer than she'd intended.

"You're amazing," he said gently when he pulled away, the stubble on his chin scratching her face slightly. She didn't mind.

She smiled, although she didn't believe she deserved the

credit. She wiggled her feet back into Todd's boots, preparing for another trek.

Jessica scooched over on the seat to the door and rolled down the window. She was becoming adept at climbing out of the window. Still, she braced herself for the iciness of the task at hand, for the hard work she was about to endure.

The snow shocked her to the core every single time. It didn't get easier. She told herself to hurry up, to get the job done. The sooner she dug them out, the sooner they could go get Todd help, the sooner she could get home. Her warm bed, her fuzzy slippers, her flannel pajamas were all calling to her. She envisioned herself tucked in, her feet toasty under the covers, maybe some hot coffee in her favorite snowman mug on the nightstand. Henry would curl up with her, and the three of them would languidly pass the next few days away recovering with the help of Netflix and Chinese takeout.

The vision drove her forward.

They didn't have a shovel or anything that could serve as an adequate digging device, so she'd have to use her hands. The thought depressed her. She needed to work fast so she didn't risk frostbite. It was still a possibility, the snow still coming down, the temperatures still dangerous.

She waded through the snow to the back of the truck and began her work. She kicked snow away from the tires, clearing as much as she could, sweat already building up. When she'd cleared some with her foot, she stooped down to begin tossing it with her hands. She aimed to imitate a digging dog, trying to fling as much snow as she could as quickly as possible.

She wiped sweat from her brow with her forearm. The work exhausted her. She'd barely made any headway when Todd yelled out the window. "Jess, you need to take a break.

It's not good to be sweating out there in the cold."

"I need to do this," she yelled back. Tears of frustration were building. This felt like the impossible task. Correction—this was the impossible task. The more she dug, the more she realized how little she'd accomplished. It was a thankless task, a discouraging task. Still, it was a necessary task.

She steadied her focus, pictured her pajamas and Henry, and stooped back down, digging some more.

When her arms felt like she couldn't toss a single snowflake and her quads screamed from the squatting position, she stood and appraised her work.

Even if the truck moved, it would only move a foot or so. It would never make it up the embankment. Unless she could make the truck levitate, they were still just as stuck as before.

Nonetheless, she had to try. She whispered a prayer into the wind, her icy lips barely moving. She turned toward the truck and trudged back to the window, to the portal into their new, bleak world.

"Let's try," she said, trying to instill conviction in her voice. Her chattering teeth and exhausted limbs made it difficult.

"Here. Put these down under the tires," Todd said, handing her the mats from the truck.

"Good idea."

"If you can pull some more branches over, that will help too. We need to get some traction."

She trudged back behind the truck, aligning the mats. She found a few tree branches and tossed them underneath the tires as well, stamping down some snow a few feet back from the tires in case they did get some traction.

"Please, God. Please, give us a miracle," she said out loud this time, her hands raised in prayer position, her face turned up to the sky, snowflakes gently careening into her cheeks, her nose, her eyelashes. She inhaled, the cold air burning her lungs, and dropped her hands. The prayer had hopefully lifted past the snowflakes to God's ears.

She marched back to the truck, exhausted but hopeful for the first time since the ordeal began.

This had to work. It just had to. Her hard work had to pay off.

***

Jess climbed through the window, lowering herself into the driver seat. She peeled off her gloves, Todd again giving her his to warm her hands. He rubbed her hands, trying to get circulation back into them.

"We need to try this. The snow is picking up again. This is go time."

Todd nodded, kissing her cheek. "You did it, baby. We're getting out of here."

"Yes, we are," she said, nodding. They needed to believe.

She turned the key, inhaling audibly. "Here we go."

She put her foot on the gas pedal and gingerly pushed it down after putting the truck in Reverse.

The tires spun, squealing angrily in the snow. The truck didn't move, the engine revving pointlessly. A ball formed in the pit of her stomach.

"Keep trying," Todd reassured. "Try going forward a little bit to get a head start. Then try putting it in reverse again."

She nodded, eyes focused on the wheel. She obeyed his instructions.

The truck still didn't budge, the sound of tires screeching

enhancing her anxiety.

Over and over, she tried, making no headway. Each time, the anger, the frustration boiled a little more.

On the fifth try, she jammed her foot down on the gas. "Dammit!" she shrieked, tears flooding her eyes. She slammed her hands on the wheel. Todd reached for her, but she shoved him away as she let off the gas pedal, knowing it had been a stupidly rash reaction.

"Turn it off. You're wasting gas we need."

"I just wasted all my fucking energy. Fuck the gas!" she bellowed at him, tears running down her face. She turned the truck off, slamming the wheel again.

"Jess, it's okay."

"It's not fucking okay. None of this is okay. It's my fault we're here. And now I tried, and dammit, we can't even get a break. We can't get a break."

"I know. Come over here. We'll think of something else. You did your best. You did good. It's not your fault. You tried. You had to try."

She crumpled against him, the exhaustion, fear, and disappointment swirling into a dangerous concoction. She cried against his shoulder, sobs racking her whole body. The disappointment, the hopelessness, the wasted effort all caught up to her. A wave of grief, of despair slapped against her like a wave at high tide. The wave stung her as it rippled through her, drenching her optimism with doubt.

"Now what?" she asked in desperation when the tears had subsided due to exhaustion. Her nose was so stuffy, it was hard to breathe. It was hard to breathe anyway, fear suffocating her, tightening her chest.

Todd wiped away the tears from her face, lifting her chin to look at him. "Now we wait. We're going to make it through this. We just have to wait."

She shook her head, leaning back against Todd's shoulder.

She didn't think she could wait another day, just sitting here trapped, hoping for a miracle that apparently wasn't coming.

Chapter Nine

As the time passed and the temperature outside dropped even more, they started to shiver. Another storm swooped over the truck, the snow and ice again pelting the windshield. The rhythmic sound intensified her frustration, made Jess feel like she was going completely mad. She wanted to shriek, to rip the cab to shreds. She wanted to break every window, to stomp into the snow and yell at God, at the truck, at herself. She couldn't take this much longer. The silent waiting game exasperated her, even with Todd there to cheer her.

She focused her energy on keeping her blood circulating. She tried to move her toes, wiggle her fingers, breathe life back into them, but it was exhausting. Her eyes drooped, fatigue and cold wearing her body down.

They'd fallen into a routine of sorts, rotating between trying to move around, resting, and turning on the truck for some heat when it got too cold. The wind thrashed outside, some loose branches cracking against the truck. The storm pounded on, only now reaching its full peak.

Too tired to talk, they huddled together, Todd stroking her arm, trying to warm her even though he shivered too. They sat, the only sign of life in the truck the billows of air coming from their mouths meeting the freezing air in the truck.

She leaned against him, and her heart stopped as a deafening bang shattered against the roof.

She jumped in Todd's arms. "What was that?"

"Probably another tree branch," Todd said in her ear. He'd jumped too.

"Are you sure?"

"No. But logic would tell me the ice and snow are weighing on the branches. I mean, unless the abominable snowman is out and about. Could be that too."

"Not funny."

"At this point, I think a yeti would be a welcome reprieve."

"So now we've got to worry about a damn tree falling on us."

Todd pulled her tighter. "It's fine. It was just a branch."

She exhaled. "If you say so."

"I say so."

Another thump happened, this time right outside her door. She screamed involuntarily, huddling closer to Todd.

"Todd, I think it's a bear," she announced, panting from fear, shivering.

"It's not a bear," he responded in an almost condescending tone, as if she were crazy.

"It could be. We're in the middle of nowhere. What if a

bear is out there, just waiting?"

"Bears hibernate."

"But it could still be a bear."

"Stop. You're being paranoid."

She shushed him, listening, waiting for the swipe of a paw on the truck. She didn't hear anything, but that didn't necessarily rule out the bear scenario, at least as far as she could discern.

Despite his quivering, he rocked her gently. Coupled with her exhaustion, his arms around her lulled her into a state of frozen serenity, even with all the fear in her heart. Her eyelids grew heavy and she started drifting away from the truck, from Todd, from the frozen wasteland they were a part of.

***

"Jess, wake up. Wake up, honey. It's just a dream."

Big hands desperately shook her, jolting her out of her own head. She snapped out of it, a cold sweat and heavy breathing slowly reminding her she had been just dreaming. The voice was right.

He pulled her close, squeezing her. "Was it the dream again?"

She inhaled slowly, calming herself like the therapist had taught her.

"Yeah," she managed.

She'd been having this dream—or nightmare, more accurately—at least once a week for the past few years. It was always the same dream.

She walked in the forest, alone, sometimes her current age, sometimes younger. She came across a bunch of faceless women, all reaching for her. They swarmed her like zombies, grabbing her, as she ran screaming.

And then the Brownsons appeared, usually wielding an ax, a machete, or some other kind of horrifying weapon.

She always woke up before they got to her, but the sheer panic of running from them, of seeing them coming after her, was enough to make her feel crazy. Even when she woke up, it usually took her a while to push the dream back down, her racing heart and labored breathing a reminder of the sheer terror of her nightmare.

"It's okay. It's just a dream," Todd murmured in her ear, wrapping his arms around her and rocking her slightly.

But the problem was, it wasn't. It wasn't completely a dream. And even now, in this life-or-death situation, it plagued her. The past never completely loosed her from its bony fingers.

***

She was five when she went to live with the Brownsons. They'd been her first foster home, and she'd been terrified.

"It'll be fine," the social worker had assured her. "They're going to take good care of you."

To be honest, Jess didn't really know what "good care" meant, looking back. Her mother had abandoned her at two, her father taking up parenting on his own. Her mom had apparently had a drug problem, even smoking marijuana when she was pregnant with Jess.

Her dad, though, wasn't any better. A cocaine addict, he worried more about getting his next fix than things like food and vaccinations and doctor appointments. She'd been taken by Children and Youth when a neighbor found Jess rummaging in her trash bags for food at the age of five.

She'd never been scared, though, living with her dad. It'd just been normal. She learned early on how to find food, who to trust and who not to trust. She learned to make an escape for herself by telling her and her single dolly stories.

Now, though, she headed to a new life, a life with the people named the Brownsons. The social worker didn't stop smiling. Jess thought it looked fake.

Pulling up to the trailer that would now be her home, she smiled at the sight out the car window. A pink flamingo statue perched in the yard. A lady stood on the porch, waving. It looked fine. It looked friendly. A young boy played in the area beside the trailer. Still, butterflies danced in her tummy at the thought of getting out of the car. She didn't know these people, didn't want to be here alone. She missed her home, the familiar walls. She missed her dad.

"Here we are, Jessica. Come on, it's okay," the smiley lady said. Jessica wanted to cry, but she just squeezed her dolly's hand. Crying wouldn't help. The woman got her out of the car, and she slowly shuffled her feet on the gravel, holding dolly's hand even more tightly. She was glad they'd let her bring dolly along.

"Hi, Jessica," the woman said from the porch. She walked down to greet them. Jessica noticed she wore soft pink slippers

*even though she was walking outside. The woman continued,
"I'm Molly Brownson. Come on, sweetie, it's okay."*

*Jess held back. The lady looked friendly enough. She wore
a sunshine-yellow T-shirt and jeans. The little boy just kept
playing in the dirt out front. A dog barked from behind the
trailer.*

*Jessica's stomach hurt. She didn't want to go in. She didn't
know why. She just kept staring at the lady's slippers, thinking
it was strange to be wearing slippers outside. She didn't know
why she fixated on them, but she just didn't want to think about
living here, staying here. Something about the place scared
her.*

*"Go on, then," the social worker said, so she did. But
she felt like maybe this wasn't a good place, not like the lady
seemed to think.*

*A few hours later, after the smiley lady had left, she quickly
realized it wasn't a good place, not at all.*

***

"If I ever saw the bastard, I'd kill him. You know that?" Todd
said, referring to Mark Brownson, the man who quickly taught
Jess that foster parents were not all loving. Todd squeezed her,
rocking her again. They were still shivering, but they'd turned
the truck on again, getting some heat back in the cab. The
warmth shocked her face, helped dry her tears. It soothed her.

Jess sighed. "I wish I could just let it go."

"No one would be able to let it go. You've done a damn
good job at it."

"Not really. Cycling through ten foster homes because you're 'difficult' isn't really doing a good job."

"Hey, now. Look at you. You rose up from that. You went to college, and now you're helping kids. You're smart and sexy, and you've got it all together."

"I try." She settled back against him, her heart finally slowing down to a normal speed.

"Plus, I mean, you're married to the golden ticket."

"Ha. I wish." She rolled her eyes, smiling despite her chattering teeth.

She didn't like to admit it, but in many ways, he was right. He *was* her golden ticket. He was the first man she'd really trusted, the first man to show her what love looked like. He was the first man to make her feel like love was possible again.

Because after Mark Brownson had abused her, she didn't trust men, not for a long time.

It had started with small things. Ordering her to do chores while Kyle, his biological son, sat and played games. Throwing a drink on the floor because it was too warm. Pitching her dolly in the trash because she was too attached.

It always happened when the smiley lady wasn't around. He never acted that way in front of the social worker, of course. He played the system expertly, and Jess was too young to question it. Plus, she hadn't really known what a healthy family looked like. She didn't think to question it.

After a while, though, the abuse ramped up, even when Molly was around. Soon, he hit her for not vacuuming well enough or for looking at him wrong or for leaving her shoes in the middle of the living room. Molly, although never abusive toward her directly, never stopped it. And so it went for a year, Jess thinking all families behaved that way, not saying a word. It wasn't until Mrs. Dobberson, her teacher, noticed bruises on her arm that things changed.

They removed Jess from the home, but more importantly, she also found her calling. She knew from that day she wanted to be a teacher so she could help kids too. It kept her focused, even as she pulled away from people, even as she became the difficult child she had a reputation for being. Through ten moves, through eight schools, she managed to stay focused on her goal. She found her way, found her independence, and found she didn't need a dolly to get her through—she was strong enough on her own. During high school, she'd learned to depend on herself, and she'd learned being rebellious wasn't the answer. She knew she needed to make something of herself, for herself, all by herself, so she could claim the life she deserved.

She didn't trust men, though, all through school. He'd shown her men were arrogant, were hurtful, were cruel. She didn't date in high school. She'd dated only one man in college, a quiet premed student who asked her out over coffee junior year. But even that failed to be a deep, full relationship. She'd been guarded, afraid that to love a man was to be hurt. Joshua hadn't shown her any signs of abuse. He'd been nothing but kind. Still, she wasn't ready to let her heart go, to open herself up to a man. The past kept beckoning her back, the image of Mark Brownson reminding her of how bad "love" could hurt.

Todd changed everything. From the moment he approached her at the wedding, she knew he was different. He was kind and amicable, loyal and dependable. As he broke down her walls, even from their first encounter, he thawed her heart. He helped her heal, helped her see what a true relationship could be. He showed her what love was. Even though they both joked and teased, sarcasm driving their humor, there was mutual, undying respect underneath it.

He would do anything for her, and vice versa. He'd unfrozen her hypothermic heart, had jolted her back to life. He'd shown her how Mr. Brownson was a monster, an anomaly, and that she wasn't at fault. She deserved better, deserved stronger, deserved love.

Todd had helped her reach out and grab it.

***

"Jess, listen. You've got to." Todd's voice was stern and direct. He peered straight into her eyes, no joking quality to his tone.

"No." She, too, was adamant.

"You're freezing. This might be your only shot."

It hurt to hear him so negative, so downtrodden. It frightened her to hear him giving up, admitting things were bad.

"I'm not going to do it. I won't leave you."

"I agree, not yet. It's risky. I don't want you out there alone. But we can't last here forever. We're freezing. The truck's going to run out of gas eventually, and we're going to get hypothermia. We don't have much food left. If things don't start looking up by the end of today, you need to get out of here, try to find help."

"No way. I'm not leaving you here to die."

"You could bring help back."

"I'm not leaving you. I love you."

Todd sighed, nuzzling against her. "I love you too. I just…. Shit, this is bad. I'm so angry that I can't do anything. I just sit here. I want to do something." She could see his jaw clenching as he slammed a fist against the door. Tears started up again in her eyes, his frustration rubbing off.

They'd survived the first night and almost survived all of today, carefully starting the truck, always praying it would actually start, each time getting iffier and iffier. She'd peeked out the window a few hours ago. Snow pelted down from the sky. They'd probably gotten another six inches. Things were getting worse. The shivering was harder to put at bay, even with the heat from the truck at ready intervals. They were growing weary, exhaustion creeping through their bones.

"We can't lose hope, not yet," she said.

He nodded, kissing her frozen hand through her glove. She moved her fingers, trying to keep circulation going. Todd grew quiet, the leg pain and the helplessness getting to him. She'd never seen him so pessimistic. It scared her. She needed to bring him out of it.

"Why don't I get out, set something up by the road? Maybe a signal?"

"I should be the one to go. I don't want you getting hurt."

"Are you freaking kidding me? You're going to try to play hero with a bum leg? Stop being sexist and let the lady save you." She nudged playfully, but he didn't smile. She knew this killed him, being helpless. She regretted her words. "Look, I've got this."

"You said the snow is bad."

"It is. But our only hope is if someone passes by and sees us."

"You're right."

"So I'm going to set up a flag of some sort. What should I use?"

"Well, I'm fresh out of flags in here. And SOS signals."

She thought for a moment, looking around her. She touched her neck, remembering the soft fabric that had cradled her skin before she'd tied it to the tree. "Perfect. I'll use my scarf. Maybe shove a twig in the ground and tie it to it by the edge of the road. Hopefully it will catch someone's attention."

He eyed her skeptically. "A scarf?"

"Hey, it's bright red. It could work." He just stared, raising an eyebrow. It did sound rather crazy, in all honesty. Still, it was the best chance they had currently. It was worth a shot, wasn't it? They didn't have any better ideas at this point.

"Okay. I've got this," she assured, mostly to convince herself. She took a deep breath. Inwardly, she wasn't sure she had it. The thought of venturing into the snow, of being soaked to the bone, seemed like a terrible idea. But it was one of the only ideas they had. The sun would soon set. With some luck, a vehicle of some sort, maybe even a snow plow, would be traveling through, would see them before dark.

She leaned over to kiss his cheek, an action for self-assurance as much as to convince him she'd be okay. She inhaled, tried to bundle her coat a little tighter, and leaned over to roll down the window.

The wind bit and the assailing snow flew into her face, knocking her breath away. She was already cold, colder than she'd ever been, but now she realized she could be much colder.

She sucked in her breath, determined to get this done. She had to. Their lives depended on it.

"Be careful," Todd said.

"Always," she muttered before lifting herself on shaky arms up to the window. Hanging out, she felt her hands slip, and she almost tumbled backward into the snowdrift. Somehow, she managed to steady herself, balancing her butt on the window as she hung on to the top of the window frame. The outside swirled in a gray menagerie of snow and ice. She tenuously swung a leg over the side of the truck and twisted around so both feet were facing the ground. She untied the scarf, grasping it as tightly as she could with her frozen hands, the red, snow-caked ends billowing in the wind. The huge branch that had fallen and startled them earlier balanced precariously on the roof of the truck. She grasped at the edge hanging near the side mirror, mustering up some strength to break a piece of the branch off. Armed with a twig in one hand, she took one more deep breath. Without more thought, without time to change her mind, she catapulted herself into the snowdrift below.

The snow caked around her, consuming her. She felt like this was it. She'd die right here.

But then she thought of Todd, about how he needed her to do this.

Fighting against the wind and snow, she crawled through

the snowdrift, eventually getting to her feet. She trudged forward, blowing snow clouding her view. She could only see a few feet in front of her and, even then, she could only see snow. Her heart sank. This was impossible.

She shivered, even more than in the cab. Her legs were leaden, the snow more like cement than the fluffy substance of her childhood snow angels. At one time, she'd thought snow to be picturesque. This experience had forever tainted her innocent, naïve view.

She talked her feet forward, begged them to cooperate. Every step felt like fifty. She didn't even know if she was walking in the right direction. It felt futile, hopeless. Even if she made it to the road, who would see this? What good would this do?

She trudged on, the branch in one hand, the scarf in the other. She stumbled and fell, her whole body encrusted in snow. Her toes were hurting. Her hands and legs were hurting. Her face ached, the wind and snow burning it with cold.

Exhaling, she knew she couldn't go much farther. Panic overtook her as she glanced back and realized she could barely see the truck anymore. This would have to do. She had failed in some ways, hadn't made it to the road. The scarf would probably never be spotted, covered in snow in a few hours' time—if it resisted the violent winds. Still, it was a try. It was her best. She'd have to have faith this would do the trick.

She anchored the flimsy branch in the snow and tied the red scarf to it. She watched it flail in the wind, the twig shaking with its movement.

Their entire life, their entire hope balanced on this slipshod signal in the middle of the embankment.

Jess couldn't help but feel like their life was being violently thrashed right along with the scarf, the wind and the elements winning the overall battle.

She didn't have time to mourn, though, at what seemed more like a tombstone marker than a signal for rescue. Frostbite worried her. She needed to get back to Todd, to get back in the truck, to dry off.

Turning, the wind at her back, she catapulted herself toward the truck, groaning with effort as she fought her way through the snow. She followed her initial tracks, making the return to the truck easier in many ways, but not emotionally.

She couldn't help but worry, wonder if this would be her last journey, her last real trek.

When she finally saw the shape of the truck, she made a last-second decision to head to the tailgate before beelining for the cab again. She stretched out her hands to feel for the truck, making sure she was in the right spot. Leaning down, she cleared the fresh-fallen snow from the back of the truck, unburying the tailpipe that had almost been covered by new snow accumulation. That wouldn't have been good.

After several minutes of kicking snow and scooping it away with her hands, she stood back, brushing the snow off her hands futilely, and studying her work. She was satisfied that at least she'd accomplished this small feat.

She felt her way around the truck, visibility still terrible, and reached the window. Looking to her right as she prepared to boost herself into the cab again, she grimaced. The scarf wasn't even visible from here, the blowing snow obstructing her view.

If she couldn't see it, surely no one else would, either. A pointless beacon, her scarf symbolized the flawed optimism they had. It was a scarlet mark reminding them how close to death they were, how close they were to the tipping point that would catapult them into the land of no return.

***

"I was so worried about you," Todd said when she crawled back through the window. She was exhausted and frozen to the bone.

"T-t-u-u-r-r-n-n he-e-ea-t…," she stuttered, her lips not cooperating.

"I've got it," he said, leaning to turn the key. The truck miraculously, thankfully, sputtered to life, and she put her wet gloves in front of the heater.

"Here, we need to get some of the wet stuff off," he said, peeling off her wet hat and laying it across the dash by the heat. He took off her coat, too, also laying it out. He shimmied out of his own coat and carefully wrapped it around her.

"T-t-o-o-o-d-d… n-n-o-o," she stammered. She didn't want him to freeze too.

"Shh. Now who's trying to be a hero? Come here. You need to get warm." He hugged her close, rubbing his hands on her. She sank into him, the heat from the truck helping slightly. She was still numbingly cold.

Despite her misery, her cold, and the threat of frostbite, she was glad she'd done what she'd done. The hope for rescue was still as limited as before her exodus. However, she noticed an uptick in Todd's mood, a new quality in his voice.

Hope. She'd helped him find hope. It was worth it, even if she knew the uselessness of her mission.

***

Time crawled, and slowly, Jess returned to a state less tenuous than when she'd returned to the truck. She was still cold, her shaking hands a blatant reminder of their predicament. Nevertheless, her body gradually warmed thanks to the heat and Todd.

He shut the truck off, to Jess's dismay. She knew they had to preserve fuel, but she hated the thought of things getting colder again when she was just starting to warm up.

They sat in silence again, both heading to a place of hope, of worry, of coldness.

When she could speak again, the dry coat and heat from the truck reviving her, she turned to Todd.

"Do you remember our wedding night?" she asked, smiling.

He was silent for a moment, so silent she thought he was done with this trip down memory lane.

"How could I forget?" he murmured a long moment later, a sparkle in his eyes telling her he was thinking it all over. He kissed her cheek, and she smiled. She leaned back against his chest, the memories floating between them. She knew they needed to hang on, no matter what. She wasn't ready to give in yet, shivering or not.

Chapter Ten

They'd said their goodbyes to the wedding guests, who were dwindling as the time passed. The fire hall had emptied, and the drinks were running dry. The cake had been cut—an ocean scene with jellyfish on top, to many guests' confusion. The garter had been tossed, even though there were only two single men in the room. They'd danced to quite a few songs, emboldened by liquid courage. Todd had carried a squealing Jess out of the reception, the cheering of the few remaining guests bringing smiles to their faces.

And now, their night as Mr. and Mrs. had begun.

It wasn't their first time. She had never taken a vow of chastity. After all, when you had over ten mothers, who was there to tell you about virginity and promiscuity and saving it?

Still, it felt magical, walking to their hotel room, husband and wife. It was something she'd dreamed of as a teenager but never thought she'd find.

But she'd found him. The sweet, dependable man who made her laugh, who was crazy enough to love her quirks. The man who made her want to let go of her past fears, who made her believe not all men were evil. The man who wanted to help her put Mr. Brownson and all of the other horrible men in her life in the past, who would die to make her happy.

"I love you, Mrs. Kling," Todd said, kissing her sloppily in the parking lot of the hotel.

"Love you, too," she said, screaming it to the sky, laughing as she did.

"Shh, it's late." He put a finger to her lips, but she just kissed it, the alcohol in her veins and the love in her heart freeing her from any worries.

They laughed wildly as Todd pulled his hand away from her lips and grabbed her by the hand. After hastily checking in at the front desk, they'd headed to the suite they'd reserved. They hadn't brought anything with them, their love for each other and intoxicated brains enough for the time being.

"Let's get this honeymoon started," Todd whispered, sliding one strap of her dress down as soon as they were in the door. He quickly kicked the door shut, reaching for her waist.

She smiled. "You know, I kind of thought we'd do something crazy first."

He raised an eyebrow. "Like what?"

"Well, there's a pool out back." She gestured with her head.

"And?"

"And... I've never been skinny-dipping."

He raised an eyebrow. "Me neither, for obvious reasons."

115

He patted his stomach, making a loud slap. She giggled.

"Stop. I love you. Let's go into this marriage with a bang."
She laughed hysterically at her choice of words.

"Fine, I'm game," he said, pulling her into him with a thud.

"I mean let's do something really memorable. Sex in a hotel? Average. Skinny-dipping on your wedding night? Exciting."

"You're such a rebel."

"I am."

"You realize no one wants to see all of this, right?" Todd asked, gesturing to his body.

"No one will. It's late. Everyone's sleeping. We'll jump in real quick, run out, and come back here."

Todd held his head. "This is absurd."

"Come on. Live a little with me."

"I think maybe I've had too many whiskeys. Because yes, let's do it."

They laughed crazily, running down the stairs toward the pool in their wedding attire. Once there, they looked at each other.

"Are we really doing this?" Todd looked around. Jess did the same. The area was clear. It was late. Surely everyone was sleeping by now. There was no harm in it. She looked back to Todd, staring into his eyes.

Jess answered him by taking off her dress. As she did, she couldn't help but notice her heart beating wildly. This was nuts. She was a wild child in her day, sure. But she didn't do this sort of thing.

Maybe she'd had too many whiskeys too.

She tossed her dress aside, and then her bra, and finally everything. Todd followed suit, a little behind her because he wouldn't peel his eyes away.

She took a deep breath, let out a shriek, and jumped into the water naked. Todd did the same, their splashes mixing with their gleeful laughter.

Jess swam a lap before swimming up to him. "Oh, that was fun."

"A little cold," Todd assessed, laughing, shaking his head. "What am I going to do with you?"

"Whatever you want," she said, kissing him.

She'd started to get into it when she heard "Excuse me?"

Her heart stopped. She'd had a lot to drink, but not enough to blow off those words. They paused, turning to a nearby gate. The hotel manager stood, clearly enraged, arms crossed.

"We got a complaint about some noise at the pool. You do know it's closed, right?" she said. Her mousey-brown lob and white collared shirt only added to her shrewdness. Jess found herself blushing.

"Sorry. Wedding night." She shrugged, putting her hands in the air and offering a smile. Surely even the mousey lady could understand, could cut them some slack. Two honeymooning skinny-dippers couldn't be the worst thing this woman had ever had to deal with, right?

"You do also know skinny-dipping is prohibited, right?"

"Um, yeah. Like I said. Wedding night."

"Well, take it to your room." The woman didn't crack a smile, her toe actually tapping.

Todd eyed Jess, winking.

"Right away, ma'am," he said, then pulled himself out of the pool. The manager shrieked, shielding her eyes, and Todd started belly laughing. Jess laughed so hard she cried. She accidentally inhaled some water, coughing and sputtering before returning to her laughter.

"I could have you two arrested, you know." The manager's voice grew louder and more intense as she tried to shield her eyes from the sight of Todd in all his glory. Jess wanted to take her seriously, wanted to apologize. She just couldn't stop laughing. Her head still felt a bit spinny, after all.

"Sorry again," Todd said, standing proudly, hands actually on his hips. He is definitely drunk, *Jess thought.*

"Just get some clothes on and get back to your room, please," the manager ordered, shaking her head as she continued to shield her eyes like her life depended on it.

She walked away, her heels quickly tapping out a rhythm on the concrete. Todd reached down to help Jess out of the pool. They gathered their clothes, haphazardly stepping into them before leaving the pool area.

They were laughing the whole way back to their room, their wedding clothes smelling like chlorine.

"Oh God, did you see her face?" Jess asked.

"I feel like check-out is going to be awkward tomorrow."

"Yeah, especially when you're sober enough to realize what you did."

"Eh, I have some Jell-O shots in my pocket upstairs. I'll throw back a couple before we head down."

"What? In your pocket?"

"Where else was I supposed to put them?"

She hit him, and they headed back to their room for what would be a memorable, loving night.

When they woke up in the morning, they looked at each other, a screaming headache dulling Jess's thoughts.

"Jess," Todd said, smiling after kissing her. "Did we...? Do you remember...?"

She laughed, throwing her head back on the pillow. "Yep. We sure did. So I'd hate to be you this morning, facing the manager. She's definitely going to be picturing you naked."

"She's probably ripped her eyes out by now."

Jess giggled before rolling over to kiss him again.

She knew from that moment that life with Todd would never, ever be dull.

***

"It's been a crazy life, you know?" he said, interrupting her thoughts.

"Sure has."

There'd been so many memories, so many wild times from that first night together. Sure, they'd fallen into the typical married rut from time to time. Dentist appointments and Netflix and flannel pajamas and spaghetti dinners sometimes took over their penchant for excitement.

But they always found a way to spice it up.

They'd been skydiving. They'd been to Tahiti once. They'd tried to live life in the fast lane as much as they could.

"It's not over yet, you know," Jess said, taking on the role of the positive voice for once. It was usually Todd's job, but a hurt leg would sometimes take the optimism right out of you.

"I hope so," he murmured, his gaze far away.

Jess fell silent, alone in a sea of worries. Maybe it was the frigidness of the night, or maybe it was the fear finally creeping in. Regardless, she decided to do something that had always calmed her, even as a little girl. She folded her gloved hands, bowed her head, and began drifting through the prayer she'd memorized so many years ago.

Todd reached to touch her hands.

"What are you doing?"

She hesitated, knowing he didn't believe in this sort of thing, knowing he likened the use of prayer to the use of some talisman. He would tell her she might as well get out her fake Harry Potter wand.

"Praying."

He didn't say anything, groaning as he shifted his weight.

"Do you want to pray with me?"

He stayed quiet, probably weighing his options. "No, you go ahead."

"Why are you so reluctant? It can't hurt anything, can it?"

"No. It can't. And if you believe it, then you pray it."

"But you don't?"

"We've been through this."

"I know. But I'd think at a time like this...."

"Jess, please. Let's not do this, not now. We need to stay strong." He blew on his hands, rocking a bit to warm up. It seemed to be just as much of a nervous gesture as a survival one. This conversation always made him uncomfortable.

"But don't you believe, just a little?" This conversation had always given her chills, but today, sitting here, things were really in perspective.

"I don't know what I believe."

"But that makes me crazy. Because I want to believe that, when I die, I'll be with you again."

"Shh, it's okay. We're not dying. We're going to make it."

"You don't know that."

They were the words that had silently been passing between them in the past few hours as the temperature got to them more and more, as the lack of food and water—other than a bit of candy and a few sips of Mountain Dew—started to play on them. As the hours of being trapped dragged on, as the hours of hopelessness dragged on, they hadn't wanted to say it out loud.

He sighed. "Look. I don't know what I believe. But if there is an afterlife, you better believe I'm going to be with you."

"What if you can't?"

"Because I don't believe?"

She shrugged.

"Then I hope you'll pull some favors with the big guy and get me in. I mean, I've got a good sense of humor. Probably would be helpful for eternity. It'll break up all the singing with the angels and stuff."

"You can't take anything seriously." She groaned, rolling her eyes.

"Nope. My point exactly." He nudged her with his shoulder, and she playfully nudged back, a simple gesture they often did when at the movies or sitting in a booth beside each other. It was a small moment, but it made her feel like things were normal, like things were okay, just for a second.

She settled back in, ready to pick up with her prayer, but she couldn't seem to focus.

She wanted to feel settled in her thought process, in her beliefs. She wanted reassurance it didn't end here, that there was more.

Because what if this was it? What if her life ended here?

She couldn't handle the thought that their story would leave off here, with this. There had to be more. There just had to.

She prayed through another few prayers. Finally, feeling frustrated, she started honking the horn repeatedly, begging for a miracle. Begging and praying and pleading with God to let them live.

Chapter Eleven

NIGHT TWO

As the gray of the day faded into blackness again and the second night fell, Jess sat in silence, fresh fear grappling with her. Todd had said they'd only needed to make it through one night, that they'd be rescued today.

He'd been wrong.

There'd been no sign of life, another storm system blowing through, making any hope of rescue null and void.

She'd pondered over Todd's words about going for help, wondering if she should be out trekking instead of sitting here. It was frustrating as hell to sit and wait. She wasn't a survival expert, but she knew going out in the elements for any length of time essentially equated to a death sentence. They were miles and miles from any type of civilization. Even if she managed to somehow travel in the right direction, with the blowing snow and her exhaustion, she would never get to help in time.

So they were sitting ducks, victims of the snow and lost miracles. They were helpless, at the mercy of nature and luck to find a way out. Depression clung to her chest. She wanted to rip her hair out at the thought of sitting mindlessly, waiting to succumb to death.

Would Todd's mom be worried by now? Would she have called again, wondering if they were okay? Would she be alerting help? Or, like so many other times, would she assume Todd and Jessica were busy, ignoring her? Would Todd's mom, their singular lifeline now, let them down, too?

Who else would notice their absence? Mrs. Pearson, the adorable neighbor lady across the street? She did keep an eye on their place, noting to Jess that she saw her come home early from school last Monday when she was sick or that she saw a pug pooping in their flowerbed out front. Would she notice their absence? Would she think anything of it?

Regardless, respite likely wouldn't come tonight. They were facing another night, another period of blackness. They were facing more freezing temperatures, more what-ifs.

The only relief she had was Todd, and she wasn't completely alone.

Tomorrow, they'd both be expected at work. Tomorrow morning, neither would show. It would raise flags, raise questions. It wasn't like either of them, especially Jessica, to go AWOL. Still, though, even if questions were asked, it's not like anyone would immediately assume they were trapped here. It had been a two-and-a-half-hour trip; the rescuers would have to cover so much territory. Even if rescuers searched the common routes from the wedding, who knew if they'd see them down here?

Who knew if they'd find them in time, if at all?

Jess rocked back and forth, her breath making plumes of smoke-like rings in the truck. She huddled tightly into herself, her arms crossed, the rocking motion lulling her into a state of neutrality. The cold, the exhaustion, the fear—it was getting the best of her. Being trapped in this tiny area, not knowing what came next, it was hard.

She wasn't one for giving up control. Perhaps it was because of her childhood. But she didn't like anyone being in charge of her destiny.

This character flaw—or strength, as she saw it—reared its head in various ways. She rarely used public transport because she didn't like her life being in someone else's hands, no matter how capable. She liked the feel of the steering wheel in her hands, even if she undoubtedly lacked skill behind the wheel. It didn't matter, though. It was the point. If her fate were to be sealed, it would be sealed by her own doing.

So sitting in the truck, mind and body numb, rocking and passing time, was excruciating. She wanted to fling open the door, run out into the snowstorm, and charge toward her fate, whatever it would be.

But she wouldn't. Because she would never leave Todd.

She would give up everything to be with him, come what may. He was her rock, her everything. Life without him was unthinkable. She'd rather die here, cold and powerless, than try her chances on her own.

She reached for his gloved hand, stroking it, rubbing it to

get circulation moving. He mercifully dozed now. She knew survival shows said sleeping in the cold was dangerous, that hypothermia could set in. But she wanted to give him a few minutes of peace, of sweet dreams of better times. The truck held a bit of heat from their last warm-up. They'd done their "exercises," which they'd been religiously adhering to every twenty minutes or so. They'd each taken a few sips of water. Her stomach growled, but they'd finished the last of the M&Ms. When Todd woke up, she'd scrounge around in the hopes her husband had hidden more snacks somewhere.

She glanced at the snoring face, mouth open, that had driven her crazy so many sleepless nights. She would give anything right now to be in their bed, kicking him softly to startle him and stop his snoring. She'd give anything to be fighting with him over the comforter or over where the "half" line fell in the bed. She'd give anything to hear the whirring fan he insisted he needed on to sleep or to see him in his ridiculous Batman pajamas he adamantly wore almost every night.

Sitting here, she realized how much she'd overlooked. She knew it wasn't anything she could be blamed for. Everyone did it—got caught up in the routine, in the chaos, in the madness. In the midst of this crisis, though, she realized the little moments were what made them who they were. The caramel-flavored coffee he made for her in the Keurig every morning before they left for work. His homemade stromboli he made every Friday night, their designated movie night at home with Henry. The sideways looks in restaurants when they were thinking the same thing about someone in their company. The laughter about the song on the radio or about their inside jokes at the grocery store or about the student nicknames they made up about the difficult children in her English class. His tendency to quote the movie *Anchorman* when she was mad to make her laugh, or their trips to Applebee's for appetizers every Saturday night. Their life consisted of a series of these small moments, and these small moments made their life great. So many times, she'd taken these days for granted, had underappreciated these beautiful times.

Sitting, freezing, in this truck, she smiled, thinking about the beautiful moments they had together every single day, moments she wouldn't take for granted if they got out of this mess. She was certain of it. It was funny, tragic how it took something like this to show you what mattered.

She was angered, frustration and helplessness coupling to create a vehement rage. This wasn't going to happen. They couldn't end like this. They hadn't built their life, found each other, spent all these years growing as a couple to end here.

She dug in her purse, finding a wedding favor shot glass with a tag on it. She plucked the tag from the glass. She found a pen and scrawled a message on it.

No Joke. Help. Route 360 and Shoehorn Road. In ditch. Kling.

She pulled the ribbon off the favor and tied it to her note. Then she reached down to the bottom of her sparkly dress and did the thing she'd never wanted to do.

She started ripping it.

She pulled and struggled, realizing her yoga class wasn't doing much for strength as she struggled to shred off a piece. She was happy, though, to be focusing her mind on something.

When it finally ripped, she smiled, laughing with happiness. Todd stirred beside her but went right back to sleep, readjusting his head on the headrest.

She tied the ribbon over and over to the piece of dress, wishing she knew how to tie a Boy Scout-level knot. She knotted, twisted, and tightened until it was as sturdy as it was going to be.

She rolled down the window a crack, gave the piece of paper a kiss, said a silent prayer, and then tossed it out the window, praying the wind would carry the dress and their saving grace to someone who would do something about it.

Tears softly fell. She knew it was ridiculous, hoping a sparkly dress would save her, tossed into the blackness and snow. But right then, tucked away in the middle of nowhere, she knew they were desperate enough to be depending on a glittery piece of fabric and a prayer.

***

"Hey, baby. Wake up," she said, gently shaking him. He didn't respond.

"Hey, Todd," she said, louder this time, her voice ricocheting in the void. He still didn't move.

Panic usurped her ability to reason, to breathe. She shoved him, shouting, "Hey," so loudly, she thought surely someone in the next town must've heard her.

"What?" he said, coming to, running a hand over his face.

She exhaled, her hand on her chest. "You scared me."

In fairness, he'd always been a deep, deep sleeper.

"Sorry, baby." He stretched his arms before rubbing the sleep from his eyes. The peacefulness he'd somehow grasped during sleep started to fade, the pain of his leg and the cold settling back in. She found his hand and dropped two pills into it once he was with it enough to not drop them.

"Here, you're due for another dose," she said. He swallowed them dry, coughing a little afterward. Once he scarfed down the pills, she asked, "How's your leg?"

"It hurts like a mother." Instinctively, he massaged his knee, wincing as he moved his leg. The branches were still in place, probably not doing much more than making it difficult to move, which was probably a good thing.

"Stupid question."

"You need to move around a bit. Warm up."

He reached for her face, pulling her in, their freezing cold lips grazing over each other's.

"That wasn't what I meant. But I like where your mind is," she whispered, leaning in to kiss him some more. They kissed languidly, feeling every sensation despite their icy bodies. She drank in the taste of him, the feel of him, the connection radiating between them. She felt the kiss more than any other kiss they'd ever shared, which had been a lot over the years.

"I love you," she whispered.

He grinned, rubbing noses with her. "Too bad our first kiss wasn't so smooth, huh?"

"Not even close."

Their first kiss hadn't been during the mac and cheese night. He'd waited until the second date. He'd turned to her at the Pizza Hut they'd gone to, leaning across the table, going in for the kiss, only to knock an entire pitcher of soda over. He'd told her later that he was sure it was finished for them, that she wouldn't be taking his calls. But she'd just laughed, got some napkins, helped clean up the mess, and then kissed him back.

It had been a simple kiss by some spilled soda and cheap pizza. It was who they were—unpretentious, happy, going with the flow.

"God, I wish Pizza Hut delivered here," he teased, readjusting himself gingerly so as not to move his leg too much.

"That would be amazing," she said. "Green peppers and onion."

"No way. Sausage, ham, and pepperoni."

"Vegetables wouldn't kill you, you know."

"And neither does meat."

"On the contrary."

"Well, it's better than other dinners we've had lately. Pretty sure you *are* trying to kill me. Dinner last Monday?"

"It wasn't bad," she said, looking at the floor.

"You almost choked to death on the pork chop you made."

"Okay, so I overcooked it a bit."

"A bit? Poor Henry drank five bowls of water."

The mention of Henry made her heart pang, but she tried to brush it aside.

"Oh, or the spoiled chicken you tried to serve me on Thursday."

"How was I supposed to know the expiration date was up?"

"I don't know, read the package?"

"Okay, Mr. Chef. You're on cooking duty from now on."

"Well, I've got Pizza Hut on speed dial. You're on."

She groaned, her role in this frequently rehearsed argument. She was, by nature, a horrific cook. She'd had quite a few foster moms who were super talented in the kitchen. Several had even tried to teach her. It just never stuck.

She'd had more kitchen disasters in their marriage than she could count. Raw Cornish hens, explosions on the stove, overspiced meats. She'd made every mistake you could make, but she never seemed to learn from them or improve. She was too unfocused for all the recipe steps and to watch meat to flip it at the perfect time.

Todd, on the other hand, was a marvelous cook. In high school, he'd worked as a cook at a diner. The problem? He was always "too tired" to cook after a day of welding. So they either choked down her sad attempts, ate chicken patties and fries, or ordered Pizza Hut. Oh, the healthy lifestyle they lived.

"You know, if I could order anything right now, you know what it would be."

"An éclair. I know. You only call me four times a week to stop and get some. What is your infatuation with them? They're not even good."

"They're amazing. Bite your tongue."

"No, they're just okay."

"I don't know. I think when I was young, I associated them with Paris, and since I always wanted to go there, I just loved them."

"You're a weirdo."

"You're just not sophisticated."

"Me? Please. I scream sophistication."

"Yeah, okay."

They settled in from their playful banter, Todd playing with a strand of her hair sticking out from his hat. The ice started outside again, assailing the already covered windshield, pinging off the top of the truck.

"Doesn't sound like it's letting up," Todd said, an air of seriousness surrounding them.

"No."

They sat for a long while, listening to the ice bouncing off the truck, listening to their hopes and dreams of eclairs and pizza and Paris bouncing right into the piles of snow.

Chapter Twelve

They sat lost in their own thought. The only reminder they were in it together was the feel of Todd's gloved hand rubbing her shoulder. Exhaustion coupling with the freezing temperatures made talking more difficult by the minute. When the cab got to a dangerous temperature, they went through their routine—wind the window down a crack, pray for a miracle, start the truck for a few minutes and circulate heat, thawing their hands and toes. Turn off the truck. Return to silence.

Fatigue suffocated Jess, and she wished she could curl up by a fireplace with a mug of hot cocoa and her favorite fuzzy slippers, watching the snow fall outside their front window, thinking about how beautiful it was.

Back home, the kids in the neighborhood would be anxious to spring out of bed in the morning, thrilled at the prospect of a snow day. They'd be sled riding and building snowmen, their gleeful shrieks filling the otherwise silent neighborhood.

Some of her own students, too old and cool for such childish pursuits, would be trudging through the neighborhood, shovel in hand, offering their services for fair compensation. She'd be checking her to-do list today, trying to accomplish as much as she could before school started up again. She'd be going over her lesson plans, seeing if everything was ready to start into *Hamlet*, revisiting her tests and quizzes like she did every year.

What would happen if…?

She tried not to let her mind go there. She tried not to think about the faces of her students when they learned of her fate, when they realized their tough but zany teacher wasn't coming back. They wouldn't fall apart without her. She wasn't the most beloved teacher in the school, but she took pride in doing a good job. She took pride in helping those students who needed it the most, the students who, like her, lacked support at home. She tried to put herself in the corner of the students who had an empty corner. She liked to think she'd touched a few lives, made them realize circumstances at home didn't define them. They hadn't defined her, in the end.

She thought of the empty desk, the confused kids, the lesson plans that would go untaught.

She felt stabbing pain at the thought that she'd never step back into the classroom again, never talk about Shakespeare and Poe and Emerson. She thought about how, when she left for the weekend, she'd been filled with exuberance at the thought of sleeping in and relaxing. Who could've known it was the last time?

She found herself grasping for hope, convincing herself

this wasn't the end. Slipping into despair wasn't going to do anything but seal her fate. They were strong. They were tenacious. If anyone could survive, they could survive. Together.

They'd had their scares before. They'd been through two bad car accidents, a tornado, a few scary illnesses. They'd been through the biggest loss of their lives when Bailey died. They'd resisted death when it called, fought their way through some impossible situations. That was what she needed to cling to now.

"Todd?" she said, her voice cracking.

"Yeah, love?"

"Do you remember when we lost her?"

A pause, ice clinking off the windshield the only accompaniment to the dark place he was probably hesitant to go.

"Yeah," he replied, squeezing her arm, stroking her hair.

Even three years later, the tears still came. The raw pain still burned.

But she'd survived it. They'd survived it.

***

All Jess could remember was the stoplight. Her eyes were fixated on it, even now, as Todd held her hand, squeezing it as she stared at the ceiling.

It had been yellow. She'd thought she could make it.

She'd been coming home from the grocery store on a Sunday afternoon. Todd was working, and she wanted to make him a special dinner. She'd been craving tacos, so she thought she'd make a fiesta for them. She was on her way home from picking up some tortilla shells and spices, nothing important. Nothing that was worth it, in the end.

It was an intersection she traveled through week after week. It was a hectic one, by their small-town standards, but she never thought twice about driving through it. She never thought something tragic could happen there.

The light beamed yellow.

She knew she should probably stop. She wasn't in a hurry. She had no reason to keep going.

But she had stomped on the gas that day, yellow meaning go instead of slow down. She'd sped through it, even as the color made the swift change to red. Her van rolled under the light when it happened. She was thinking about how many tablespoons of cumin she should put in the mix when her world upended.

And that's when the minivan that had been in a hurry, the minivan that hadn't expected someone to be running a red light, kept pummeling down the road.

Metal screeched, and the feeling of being tossed around like a rag doll in a Tilt-a-Whirl consumed her. The spinning, the flying, the searing pain. Her head seemed to shatter into a million pieces, the sound ricocheting right off her brain.

And then, after an eternity, there had been nothing.

Now, the nothing feeling, the empty blackness, returned to her heart.

She'd survived, despite plenty of stitches and a concussion. Physically, she would recover.

But the baby—she was a different story. She'd been too young to survive such an early birth. She wasn't viable, the doctors had said. The force of the crash had been too much.

With those words, Jess felt like her own life wasn't viable.

She'd killed their baby. She'd killed their baby over a stupid dinner plan and a split-second decision. Her reckless choice had ended in the death of their daughter.

She was an even worse mom than her parents had been. She was worse than the Brownsons. She was the worst human being on the planet. She just simply wanted to die.

***

The months after Bailey Kling, as they'd named her, passed away had almost torn them apart. They'd obliterated the Jess she'd been. She'd taken a year off work, sending them into financial despair. She didn't care, though. It took everything in her to keep breathing. She couldn't handle work, couldn't handle facing the pitying looks, the thought that her daughter would never make it to high school English.

Todd had been there, holding her hand the whole time. Never once had he blamed her or asked her what she'd been thinking. He never held it against her, never asked her why. He'd held her hand from the moment she woke up in the hospital until the moment they'd set the casket in the ground. He'd held her hand after that, on the nights when she paced in the living room, unable to sleep because of the shrieking agony in her mind. He held her hand when she told him she thought about killing herself, that it was too much.

He held her hand once a week during visiting hours when he came to see her at her inpatient program at the hospital after the grief became debilitating. He tried to soothe her, to reassure her, to love her. Through it all, he'd never stopped loving her.

He held her hand after her release, when his family members scorned and sneered at her, when friends suddenly weren't friends anymore.

After the weight had stopped crushing her chest every second, after she learned to forgive herself, she had to start the grief cycle all over again. She felt guilty for the burden Todd was left with. He'd lost a daughter, too, but she hadn't been there for him. She'd been so consumed by her own sorrow, she'd left him to suffer on his own.

But Todd was strong. He'd stood, a pillar in their relationship, holding down the fort until she could come back to him. They'd cried, they'd mourned, they'd asked why.

Bailey hadn't been planned. She'd been an unexpected miracle, one that made Jess afraid. When she'd first found out, she'd been terrified, afraid of what the word "mother" meant, afraid she didn't know how to be one. How could you be a mother when you didn't ever really have one?

Once it sank in, once the baby clothes started filling the closet of their spare room and she started picking out paint colors and taking breastfeeding classes, the fear subsided. She could do this. Todd would help her. They'd be okay.

After they lost their angel baby, though, she'd fallen back into doubt. Maybe she wasn't meant to be a mother. Maybe God took Bailey because she wasn't going to be a good mother.

The grief never went away. Even today, they treaded cautiously when talking about children. She'd held on to hopes. They'd recently been exploring the idea more deliberately.

Now who knew if they'd get the chance.

The ache in her chest over Bailey and over this void was unbearable.

"We're never going to be parents," she said to Todd. He rocked her, knowing she was replaying the same awful day he was. They didn't need to talk about it. They'd both replayed the day over and over for the past several years.

They'd learned to live through it. They'd built a life after the sadness. They'd had fun, crazy moments. They'd smiled. They'd let themselves dream again.

But Bailey never strayed far from their thoughts, not really.

"Shh, hey now. Yes, we will."

"Todd, be real. We're not getting rescued."

"Let's be real. We've been through so much together. We've survived so many horrible things, so many tragedies. Remember how we felt? We felt like surely we wouldn't make it. But we did. This is another one of those times. This is nothing, really. Someday, we're going to tell our children about this crazy story, about the time we were stranded, about how we made it through together. We're going to have this wild-eyed little girl with frizzy black hair jumping up and down, asking us to tell it again. We're going to have this redheaded little boy sitting right beside her, holding his mama's hand as he listens to the snow story."

"At least if we don't make it, I'll get to see her. I'll get to tell her I'm sorry…." Jess started sobbing, the racking sobs of a mother who has lost her child.

"Hey, shh, come on. You're going to hold her again someday, baby. But not today. Not tomorrow, either. Not for a long time," he whispered, his face moistened with tears too.

They rocked gently, the memories and pain still strong. Finally, she wiped away the tears, like she'd done so many times.

"You're right. We're going to survive this. We just have to."

"There's my girl," he said, kissing her cheek.

They were going to survive.

Chapter Thirteen

The hours dragged on. They took turns resting, humming songs, and sipping some water. They took turns hoping for miracles, talking about what they'd do when they got home, cheering each other. They searched the truck gingerly, being careful not to jolt Todd's leg too much, the pain still wearing on him. She'd found a mint underneath the driver seat. It was of questionable origins and date, but they'd carefully split it in half. An old, potentially moldy mint never tasted so damn good.

Without Todd, Jess knew she would've given up by that point. He was her solace, her companion. Now she knew that more than ever.

They weren't as chatty, weariness and cold and the horrible feeling of shivering getting to them. They were dying for warmth, for hope, for survival.

Her mind traced their steps, their relationship, stepping

through time to happier moments. It was like a scrapbook had opened before her, and she perused the pages.

Despite some hardships, despite the horrific loss, it'd been a good life so far.

The wheel of memories landed on one in particular from their first year of marriage, and she started laughing.

"What could possibly be funny right now?" he asked.

She kept giggling. "I was thinking about the time... you know the time... when we...." Her laughter kept bursting through her words, and he was finally laughing too.

"Let me guess. You're talking about the time you almost got us arrested on the beach, right?"

It was not one of their finer memories. In fact, it was so bad, even Todd didn't bring it up when he was going through his random discussion of funny moments at gatherings with friends and family.

But it was one of her favorite memories because it was one of the first times she actually saw Todd speechless.

***

"Look how gorgeous the waves are right now," Jess said, staring out at the ocean, the curtains flapping in the wind on their balcony.

He stepped behind her, wrapping his arms around her, kissing her cheek. It was late, really late. The beach was empty, the gulls' cries and the sounds of laughing children gone away for the night, resting for another day of beachy bliss. The moonlight cast an eerie glow on the water, like a scene from a movie.

They'd been out to a bar a few blocks behind the hotel,

*singing karaoke and enjoying one of the last nights of their
vacation with a beer and a margarita. Now she stood, wistful,
staring out from their hotel room balcony.*

"What are you thinking?" he asked, grinning.

"I'm not."

*"You've got that look on your face," he said. "That
familiar look."*

*"What look is that?" she asked, his beard tickling her
neck.*

*"Trouble. That's what it is." He kissed the crook of her
neck, and she involuntarily shivered like she always did.*

*She giggled. "I was thinking about how we should cross
something off our bucket list."*

"I didn't know we had one."

*"Yeah, of course we do. It's got all the traditional things on
it. You know, skydiving, tattoos, the Grand Canyon."*

*"Okay. So you want to get a tattoo? Is that what you're
saying? I think three in the morning might not be the best time.
Pretty sure only some pretty sketchy places will be open."*

"No. I was thinking of something else."

"What's that?"

*She shrugged, holding back. Finally, she blurted out, "Sex
on the beach?"*

He started laughing. "Really?"

"I knew you'd think it was stupid."

"No, no. I just…. Wow. I don't know."

*"Come on. It's our last night here. Let's do something
memorable."*

*"Sand in my ass crack, potential drowning hazard, and
potential onlookers. Sounds romantic."*

"It's late. No one is out. And we'll take beach towels."

"Oh, wow. The privacy."

"The beach down here isn't crowded anyway."

"I don't think it's a good idea," he murmured, hesitation in his voice. "Remember our wedding night?"

"How could I forget? It's one of my favorite memories. Let's make another memory. Come on. Live a little," she replied, nudging him with her elbow.

He groaned. "Dammit, if you weren't gorgeous, I'd tell you no."

She smiled. "Away we go, then, captain," she said, pulling him behind her.

They trudged silently down the stairs and through the lobby, not a soul in sight. They had their beach towels in hand. She ran ahead in the sand, laughing as the night wind tossed her hair around like it was nothing.

The tide was high so they couldn't go too far onto the beach.

"What if we get swept away?"

"Then we'll have a wonderful story to tell."

"To whom? I'm not sure beachside sexcapades are appropriate stories to tell Grandma over Christmas dinner."

"Shut up and kiss me. We're supposed to be making this quick," she said, leaping into his arms and wrapping her legs around his waist.

He obliged, kissing her hard and fast. In no time at all, they were slinking to the ground, a towel spread out.

They were undressing quickly, laughing like two rebellious teenagers. Groping each other to get things started, they froze when a light flashed on them.

Jess and Todd shielded their eyes, trying to make out what was happening, both scrambling to cover up.

"And what do we have here?" a stern voice asked. Boots on the boardwalk walked toward their spot on the sand. "Looks like we have illegal trespassing as well as indecent public exposure, huh?"

Jess's heart stopped. Todd muttered, "Shit."

They both stood to face the law, scrambling to cover themselves with the strewn clothing, the excitement of the sandy rendezvous suddenly distant.

"Officer, hi. I'm so sorry. This is all my fault," Jess stepped in, hoping her way with words would get them out of this mess as she slinked back into her shirt.

"Didn't you read the signs, miss? Absolutely no one on the beach after midnight. Absolutely no sleeping on the beach. And, well, this whole little scenario is always illegal."

"Please, sir, we're sorry. We're from out of town. We're newlyweds, actually."

Todd stood silent, practically holding his breath. Jess continued on. "And I thought, well I thought it looked like a beautiful night, don't you think? And we came down, and I got, well, ahead of myself. He tried to tell me it was a bad idea."

"Yeah, it was a bad idea." The officer approached them, shining the light on Todd. "Are you on anything out here?"

"No sir, oh my God, no," Jess spoke for him. Todd shook his head but still didn't say a word, frozen. Jess turned to him, realizing he stood speechless. His face was so pale. His eyes

were fixed on the handcuffs on the officer's hip.

"We're so sorry. We'll go back to our hotel, and you won't hear from us again."

"Well, the problem is, I haven't heard from him at all." The officer motioned toward Todd with the flashlight.

Jess turned to Todd again, waiting for him to jump in, to help her out. He just stood, motionless.

"Sir, are you okay?" the officer asked, more sternly this time.

Todd nodded.

The officer approached him, shining the light in his eyes. "Pupils look normal," he observed.

Jess nudged Todd, willing him to snap out of it. He looked like he was drugged.

"Sir, I need to ask you something, and I need you to respond. Are you here against your will?"

"What? Oh my God," Jess shrieked. The officer held up his hand to shush her.

Todd stood for a long moment. Jess's jaw dropped. What the hell was he doing?

"N-n-no, sir."

The officer looked at Jess and then at Todd again. "All right, I'm going to let you off with a warning this time. But I better not hear from you two again."

"Thank you so much," Jess said, pulling Todd toward the hotel.

Once the officer left, Jess exhaled. "What the hell, Todd? What was that?"

"I just.... I freaked.... I thought...."

Jess laughed. "You're ridiculous. Mr. Rough and Tough, and you freeze up around an officer."

He was coming around, calming down. "Shut up or I'll go tell him you did, in fact, kidnap me."

"That was ridiculous."

"So, sex on the beach left unchecked, I guess?" he asked.

"There's always next year," she said, winking.

"I think I'll pass."

"We'll have to go to a different beach, that's all."

"Are you trying to get me arrested, woman? I mean, skinny-dipping on our wedding night, and now this? We're not doing so well at this whole getting kinky in public thing. Maybe we should retire our bucket list."

"Maybe." She winked again, pulling him into the elevator. "You know, sex on the beach was a no go, but sex in an elevator...."

"Stop it, woman."

"Don't call me that."

"Man, then?"

"You're impossible."

She pulled him in, picking up their kissing right where they left off.

They did manage to cross one thing off their bucket list that night, the emergency stop button helping them stay out of too much trouble.

***

"You were so embarrassing."

"I thought he was going to arrest me."

"So you just freeze up? That'll help things. He thought you

were stoned."

"I… I panicked, okay. Not my finest moment."

"Obviously."

"But hey, I made up for it in the elevator, right?"

She held her hand up, giving a so-so gesture.

"You're cruel."

"You almost let a police officer think I kidnapped you."

"Okay, I'll give that to you. What the hell was he thinking? Look at us. How the hell did you kidnap me?"

"With my charm and siren song."

Todd shook his head, rolling his eyes.

"I am sad, though," she said. "We never did cross sex on the beach off our bucket list."

"I think it's a little overrated. Sand in the crack is never a good thing."

"You are the most unromantic man I know."

"I'll own that."

"Can I ask you something serious?" she said, turning to look at him. He nodded. "Did you get everything you wanted?"

"What do you mean?"

"I mean in life in general. Did you get everything you wanted?"

He sighed. "We're going to make it."

"I know. But I just…. I'm curious. Did you do everything you wanted to do? Did life turn out like you wanted?"

He sat in silence, playing with his facial hair mindlessly as he did. "Growing up, I wasn't really sure what I wanted in life. I wasn't like you, focused on goals. For me, life's always about being happy. Finding a sliver of happiness in the chaos. So yes, I got exactly what I wanted. I got an amazing woman who makes me laugh, makes me live, makes me crazy sometimes, but really makes life worth it. I've got a decent job, a house I'm proud of, and I got to do some pretty cool stuff. Obviously, there's still stuff I sort of want. I mean, a yacht and a million dollars would be nice. I wouldn't turn it down."

She nudged him in the ribs.

"What? I wouldn't turn it down. But am I happy? Yes. Would I trade this life? No way. Because, Jess, what we have, it's magical in its own way. Sure, it's not super romantic and fancy and the quote, unquote 'high-life.' But it's ours. And I love it, every piece of it."

"I love you, too," she said.

"Now this whole scenario, I could do without—the whole freezing, shattered leg bit. I love spending time with you, but God, woman, I'd rather you have locked me in the coat closet with you or something. This is a little bit of overkill."

She smiled at his words, nodding, before getting serious. "We have a good life. We do. I'm glad I got to spend it with you."

He didn't stop her, didn't correct her and say they had so much time left. He just nodded.

Because deep down, he probably thought the same thing.

This could be it. This could be all they got.

It had been a good life. They'd had so many beautiful moments, so much to be thankful for.

Still, she personally had so much left unfinished. They had so much left incomplete as a couple. They would be leaving this world not even half-done, a bucket list mostly untouched, and a life not fully lived.

Chapter Fourteen

There was so much left to do.

It was something Jess always felt, even in day-to-day life.

Laundry that didn't get finished. Lesson plans that needed to be fixed. Quizzes to grade, dinner to cook, curtains to wash, sit-ups to do. Her days were endless swirls of busy.

Now, though, the fear of death settling its ugly self in, she realized these were not the tasks to worry about. These were not the unfinished items she would go into the great unknown thinking about, contrary to what she used to think.

The dreams left undone were what haunted her most, the things she thought she had so much time to accomplish.

The manuscript sat, four chapters complete, on her desk in the corner of their spare bedroom, the pen's indentations scarring the paper with her thoughts. It wouldn't be finished; her words wouldn't be completed. Her story would be left to gather dust.

It's not that she expected it to go anywhere. It was a pipe dream from her childhood, an inspirational quote poster in her room telling her to "dream big" the only reason she'd even toyed with the notion. And Todd, of course.

As a middle schooler, she'd loved putting pen to paper. In a life of chaos and uncertainty, she liked leaving something permanent, some sense of emotion behind. She'd carried several journals with her house to house, filled with musings of a young mind, a broken soul, a shattered girl. But when she'd grounded herself in reality, when she'd found her purpose and focus, she'd stopped. It felt senseless to live in the made-up pages of her words. It felt wasteful.

Still, the dream never left. She'd sometimes daydream about the day she could touch her book, the one with her name on it, on a shelf. She dreamed of the day those people who'd told her she was trouble or a disaster or not worth their efforts would see her name on the bookshelf, would see her words resonating with others.

She dreamed of a day when Jess wouldn't be just some foster girl's name. It would be the name of the girl who could, who did.

She rested her head on Todd's shoulder, the ice still stabbing at her. He was quiet, probably lost in his own thoughts too. The cold crept back in, but she knew they were getting low on gas. They needed to preserve, to hold out. The key was to hang on as long as they could. If they could make it another day or two, maybe someone would find them. Maybe....

The word tossed her back into her regrets, the thoughts of her manuscript sitting on her desk plaguing her.

Maybe.

The word held so much. Hope, fear, regret. It held potential, possibility, and dreams.

Maybe she could've finished it.

Maybe she could've become a published writer.

Maybe she could've achieved her dream.

But maybe not.

She gritted her teeth, frustration overpowering her fear. Anger boiled inside her. Was this the universe's cruel joke? It taunted her with all these possibilities for a happy life to end it... here? With so much left undone? What had been the point?

She wanted to focus on all the beauty, on all the good. It *had* been a good life. She'd been lucky in so many ways.

But now, with her fingers and toes numb, with her body chilled to the bone, she couldn't help but think of all her regrets, all of the incompletes.

She would never know if her book could've been published. She would never have her legacy carried on in the faces, personas of her children. She would never go to Little League or dance recitals with Todd, taking way too many pictures of their little one. There would be no candy collecting at parades, school parties, graduations. There would be no more anniversaries celebrated together, no more bucket list rendezvous. There would be no more wild vacations or concerts or spur-of-the-moment trips to local places.

There would be no walking their daughter down the aisle or standing beside their son as he teared at the sight of his bride. There would be no holding of grandchildren, reminiscing, or passing on their wisdom. There'd be no more dream chasing, life living, or memory making.

There were so many moments she'd thought were guaranteed.

Now she realized nothing was guaranteed. Life could be going along at a humdrum pace, promising you forever. And then a single moment could rip everything to shreds. A single choice, a single movement of your foot on the brake could obliterate everything you thought you had time to do.

A single tear ran down her cheek, partially from anger, partially from sadness. She looked at their lives and saw so many future moments floating into unreachable wisps, the visions clouding into unattainable dreams.

She took a deep breath. She always believed everything had a purpose, that everything happened for a reason.

But why this? What was the point of this?

"Todd?" she said, her voice cracking.

"Yeah?" he responded, a solemnity in his.

"I'm scared. I don't want to die."

A lengthy pause ensued. She waited for him to squeeze her close, for him to reinstate those wispy visions of tomorrow.

But instead, he reaffirmed her wildest fears. "I'm scared too."

The tears flew freely, soaking her gloved hands as she tried to wipe them away.

All of the what-ifs of tomorrow, all of the possibilities of their dream were being buried with every snowflake falling from the sky.

Todd reached over and honked the horn twice, a pleading

cry in the wilderness, with a higher power, for redemption.

But redemption and safety didn't answer their plea, only the pelting of more ice.

Chapter Fifteen

"I'm worried about him. Who will take him?"

Todd clasped her hand, trying to force some life back into it. It was pointless. She couldn't even feel her hands anymore. He didn't have to ask her who she was talking about. It was all she talked about, even on good days.

Henry.

The dog she hadn't even wanted, the dog who had stomped into her heart with his mastiff paws. He was her best friend, other than Todd—sometimes maybe even more than Todd. His soulful brown eyes reminded her how exciting, meaningful life could be. Even on her worst day, he was there, snuggling with her, his droopy head on her shoulder.

Now all she could think about were his sad eyes watching the door, waiting for them to come home. She pictured him with his stuffed zebra toy, his favorite that she'd gotten him his first Christmas. He would lie there, wondering where they were, wondering why they'd abandoned him.

It was too much to think about. The thoughts of the destroyed future, the thoughts of her death, they tortured her.

The thoughts of Henry waiting for them forever massacred her heart. How could he understand? He would think they abandoned him. He would forever be waiting by the front door for her to come home, to watch television with him, to feed him cupcakes and kiss his huge black nose.

"My mom will take care of him," Todd whispered into the air between them, a chilling statement meant to soothe her. It only broke her heart even more.

"But she doesn't even know him like we do. She doesn't know he's afraid of ceramic tile or how he won't pee if there's a squirrel in the yard. She doesn't know he will only take his heartworm pill if you coat it in peanut butter. She doesn't know him."

It was irrational. She felt like a psycho, sobbing about a dog. She could blame the emotional stress from the tragedy, could say it was hypothermia settling into her brain.

But it wasn't.

She loved that dog. The thought of never seeing him again ripped her heart out. The thought of him waiting until his dying day for them to come home, wondering why they'd never come back for him, shook her to the core.

"Baby, it's going to be fine. He knows we love him. Mom will take care of him. It's going to be okay. Henry will be okay."

"No, he won't." She was inconsolable now. It was just one more thing this accident was taking, one more life ruined.

She slammed her hands on the steering wheel, laying on the horn.

"Stop," Todd said, pulling her back. She fought him, and he groaned, twisting his leg as he tried to calm her down. She regained her composure.

"I'm sorry."

"I know. It's okay. Listen, we're not giving up, right?"

She didn't answer. He didn't prod her for once. They both knew every minute that ticked by, their situation got more precarious. The snow persisted, the storm not letting up. Each moment, they were getting further and further buried in a mountain of snow, in an icy, suffocating coffin. Little traffic traveled this road. Even if their family did send out rescuers, how long would it be until they found them?

Their hopes were resting on a red scarf probably no longer visible and a note tossed into the wind.

A too familiar melancholy settled between them again. She tried to distract herself from the thought of Henry. She tried to think of practical things—lesson plans, the laundry in the dryer that needed to be folded. She thought about what she'd eat as soon as she got home, how she'd say screw this newfangled diet. It was stupid anyway.

The silence haunted them, but they'd grown accustomed to it.

So when they heard a rumbling, it startled them. A scraping noise accompanied the low rumble. It sounded distant. She thought she'd invented it.

"Holy shit," Todd said, scrambling for the horn. He honked it over and over, the promising, distant noise animating him.

Paralyzed by disbelief, Jess didn't move. Quickly, though, she swung into action. She rolled down the window, noting a lot more snow on the side view mirror. Like an acrobat, she tossed herself up onto the window seal and turned her legs, jumping into the bank.

"Help, please," she screamed, desperation driving her through the snow. She waved her arms, jumping and screaming.

The snow flew down, but as she scrambled toward the embankment as fast as she could, the creator of the noise came into hazy view.

A snowplow—the most glorious sight she'd ever seen.

Todd still honked the horn, and she screamed, flapping her arms. She was so far from the road, but she couldn't stop. This was their chance. This could end it all.

She dashed, still screaming, as the plow truck roared down the road.

It had to hear them. It would see them, would save them.

But as she continued running toward the road, the deep snow making the task almost impossible, it whirred past. Her heart stopped. It was clearly pulling to the side, finding a safer place. That had to be it, she reassured herself as she kept stomping through the snow, yelling, hands waving.

She kept running even when the sound of its plowing became distant, barely audible even in the silence of the snowstorm.

Maybe it was going to get more help. It was probably rushing to get help, to bring back rescuers. That had to be it, she thought.

The truck horn continued blaring as Jess stood, gaping at the road, still only halfway up the embankment. She stood staring in disbelief until the noise of the snowplow wasn't even a distant whir anymore, was nothing more than a hazy memory

She wasn't one to give up easily. But if she had a gun, she would've ended it right then. Because the tease of rescue coupled with… this… was too much. The hopelessness she'd felt before paled in comparison to the feeling of a rescue slipping away.

Tears fell down her cheeks. She was numb and wet for nothing. She'd probably get frostbite for sure now, but it didn't matter. None of it mattered. It was over. It seemed they were destined to die here, freezing, miserable, desperate.

Up ahead, she saw the red scarf, still tacked down somehow. Snow packed it to the ground, it's blowing freedom overpowered by the suffocating white powder.

She stomped toward it and let out a wild cry that sounded more like a yeti than a woman. She grabbed the scarf from the ground and, still letting out a war cry, attempted to shred it into a million pieces, just like her heart.

When she couldn't, she tossed it as far as she could into the snow.

"Fuck *everything*," she shrieked. She slumped back to the truck, her feet moving even more slowly now, the horn still blaring. Instead of a resonating, musical note, it sounded like a blaring alarm, a death wail. Todd was still living in the dreamworld where safety and rescue were only a horn honk away. She'd have to shatter it for him, to tell him they were done. She'd have to drag him back to the murky abyss with her where they didn't get rescued, where they died in the cold cab of a truck in the middle of an icy hell.

The cold had finally seeped the entire way through to her core, to her heart. It was black, not with fear but with the feeling of giving up.

Chapter Sixteen

They didn't say a word. Todd had stopped honking, had turned to her as she slithered back into the truck a frozen mess. He'd helped her take off the wet clothes, a routine too familiar to them at this point. He'd hugged her close, starting the truck and warming her by the vent.

He didn't ask for an explanation.

Her posture, her face, her lack of words expressed it all. She stewed in feelings of the darkest despair yet.

"Maybe they'll come back," Todd said an eternity later.

She didn't respond.

"Maybe my mom's figured something is up. Help is probably on the way."

She still didn't respond.

She couldn't. She was tired of this charade. She didn't want to pretend anymore. They were dying. She may as well succumb to it. They were dying in a frozen tomb, encased in regrets and fear. They were dying on a goddamn mountain on the way home from a wedding they should've never gone to.

They were dying together in this truck, but did it matter? Together, alone… they were dying. And there was nothing they could do. Not even their love, especially not their love, could save them.

She brooded for a while, and Todd let her, apparently sensing her anger, perhaps feeling it himself. It was a long, icy while before he spoke.

"Disney."

She wanted to ignore him, but the feelings of disappointment were slowly dissipating, if only because she was too tired to hang on to them any longer.

"What?"

"Disney. That's where I most want to go if we survive this."

She noticed an important point. He used the word "if." She was angry at him for still pretending they had a chance, but at least he was a little more realistic. He used "if," so she would play along, she decided.

"Disney? Really? So cheesy."

"We could go to Universal Studios too. Tell me you don't want to see Harry Potter World."

She smiled. "Okay, that would maybe be a little cool."

"Butterbeer and Diagon Alley? A little cool?"

"Very cool."

"Okay. Your turn."

"My turn what?"

"Your turn to add to our 'if we don't fucking die' bucket list. Go."

She squeezed his hand, smiling at his title. "Africa."

"Africa? Okay, explain."

"I've always wanted to go on a volunteer trip to teach English in one of the small schools there."

"Sounds dangerous."

"Really? We're freezing to death, and you're worried about some elephants and lions?"

"Truth. I guess I could help weld something or whatever."

"I'm sure we'll find something for you to do."

"My turn. Photography class. I want to be able to take better pictures."

"I'm awesome at selfies. I don't need a photography class." She turned to wink at him and give him her best duck-face impression. He rolled his eyes.

"Just trust me, you do. Half the time you cut my head off."

"On purpose. Okay, next up—ballroom dance lessons." She felt her face soften, the disappointment leeching back out of her. She looked at Todd, his face scrunched up at her current addition to the list.

He groaned dramatically. "So clichéd. And not my style. How did we go from dangerous African adventure to something so boring?"

She nudged him playfully. "Your turn. What are you waiting for? This was your depressing game," she chided him, but he didn't respond for a while. The stiff silence pranced in the truck, elevating the seriousness of the moment.

"I just want to enjoy every moment. Everything we took for granted. God, Jess, we took so much for granted. So many little things. I want to get the chance to enjoy them."

She nodded. "I think that's the only thing we need on the bucket list."

He leaned in to kiss her cheek, his icy lips not physically warming her. However, the love radiating between them thawed her impossibly frozen heart, shot life back through her veins.

She loved him. He loved her. Theirs was not the love of fairy tales. It might not end with the prince saving the princess, but it was their love story, and it was beautiful to her right then despite the depressing realities and fears.

It was simply beautiful, the two of them together, no matter what happened. She would die, whether it be today or in one hundred years, thinking they were beautiful together.

Chapter Seventeen

She didn't think they could make it another night.

The thought scared her out of her mind, but it was reality. They were starving. They were freezing, weakness and fatigue wearing on them. Plus, Todd was quieter now, his face contorting more frequently. Even the painkillers weren't helping. His leg was not in good shape, not at all. She worried complications were going to bring him down.

They needed help. Days with a hurt leg would be dangerous in a normal situation. Almost three full days with a hurt leg in this kind of atmosphere was downright deadly, especially since neither really knew exactly how bad it was. The way it looked, though, she knew it wasn't good, even if she wasn't a doctor.

She shuddered, not wanting to go there. She couldn't imagine a life without Todd. He was her rock, her everything. Her life had been shadowed by failed relationships, disappointments, and letdowns by other people. Her entire life, she'd been unknowingly searching for stability, for connection, for love. She'd found that with the jeans-wearing man at that wedding years ago. Now she didn't think she could survive without it.

Before Todd, she'd been a scrappy girl, fighting her way through life. Despite her empathetic nature, she'd been stoic and independent. She hadn't needed anyone or anything to get by. She'd learned to fend for herself.

Sitting here in this situation, though, she realized how much things had changed. Half of her heart no longer resided in her body; it resided in the man beside her. He'd nurtured her back to being a trusting, connected woman. He'd shown her not every man would hurt you or let you down.

He'd shown her what true love looked like.

A life without Todd wouldn't just be a return to the coarse, untrusting girl she once was. It would be true death, a loss of everything she was. She wouldn't do it, couldn't do it.

He needed to hang on, and if he couldn't, she needed to clutch on to him with everything she had. She could not let him go. They were in this together, just like everything else. Live or die, they were in it together.

She threaded her arm around his, snuggling closer, humming a song.

Their song, the first song they danced to: Faith Hill's "Breathe."

He stirred then, coming out of his thoughts, out of his pain, to smile.

"That's a pretty good song," he whispered.

"Yeah, it is."

"Dance with me?" he asked, grinning.

"Okay."

Sitting in the truck, side by side, they danced, swirling around the garden back home. He twirled her near the roses, the sun warming her back, beaming into her eyes. She didn't squint, didn't try to block it away. Instead, she danced with Todd, the beauty of the moment making her smile.

It was a beautiful thought, so beautiful she felt instantly warmed by the idea of it. She squeezed his hand.

"I love you, forever."

"I love you longer than forever."

Longer than forever.

She liked the sound of that.

She drifted to sleep on his arm, knowing when she woke the blackness would again be taking over. It was okay, though, because for right now, she sat beside Todd, the memories of their imaginary dance still lingering, still warming her body and soul.

Chapter Eighteen

NIGHT THREE

Todd blew on his hands, and Jessica rolled her eyes.

"Will you just take your turn already?" she demanded, throwing a piece of the Chex Mix into her mouth as he continued his theatrics.

"The whole game rides on this roll."

"And spitting on the die is going to help?" She laughed at his dramatic gesture as he made a scene again.

It was a quiet Friday night, just the way they liked them. The holidays had come and gone, the tree still lit up in the corner of the living room. Henry slept by it now, still worn out from the week's festivities. Jess and Todd still had unwrapped boxes strewn about the tree, presents still waiting patiently to be stowed away.

But not tonight. They had more important things to do

tonight than organize or clean up Christmas remnants.

They had a Yahtzee tournament.

It had started during their dating years, a love for Yahtzee passing from Todd to Jessica. They were competitive by nature, and the game only amped up the tendency.

"Dammit!" Todd yelled, examining the die. "It's your fault. You rushed me."

She grinned at his feigned anger, eating more Chex Mix, tossing a piece at his face.

"Really? You think it's funny? Sabotaging my roll? That's it." He leaped out of his kitchen chair, grabbing the bowl of Chex Mix with one hand.

Then he did the unforgivable. He dumped it over her head, shrieking like a five-year-old boy who'd just tossed his first water balloon.

She sat in crumbs, stunned, holding her hands out. "Are you freaking kidding me?" Anger boiled over. She wanted to choke him.

She rushed him, standing to poke at him, hit him, shove him, anything to take out her anger.

"I'm going to kill you," she screamed, and he only laughed louder, racing through their home. She chased him through the living room, up the stairs, his laughter only making her angrier.

"What an ass. I'm covered in crumbs. You're so damn immature," she bellowed down the hallway as he rushed into their bedroom. When she caught up to him, he grabbed her wrists, holding them, only making her madder.

Why did he have to be so strong?

He guffawed, out of breath from their run and his laughter.

"That was the best," he said, choking a little from all the laughing.

"I hate you," she said, trying to fling her crumb-filled hair in his face.

He pulled her in tight. She tried to slip away.

But the way he pulled her in, the way his warm body melded perfectly against hers, her anger dissipated, to her chagrin.

He'd covered her in Chex Mix. She should want to kill him. Still, despite her anger, she found her lips searching for his, found herself easing into his hands.

The mood shifted, his kiss warming her frozen, angry heart. They fell onto the bed together, hands tugging at clothes, the Yahtzee competition soon forgotten.

They basked in each other, hungrier for each other than they'd been their first time. They kissed, touched like two people who were just discovering each other, yet also like two people who'd been together for years.

They walked the balance between new and the familiar, smothering themselves in a perfect, genuine, deep kind of lovemaking.

When they collapsed into the sheets, catching their breath, she turned to look at him. His eyes sparkled, and he wiggled his nose.

"You know, it would be nice if before we make love, you'd shower now and then. I'm all for lax hygiene, but gosh, your hair is so gritty. Gross." He winked at her after he put extra emphasis on the last word.

She scowled, hitting him hard on the chest. "I still hate you."

"Not what you were saying a minute ago."

"There are damn Chex crumbs all through our bed now."

"Yeah, I'm thinking we'll be pulling Chex Mix out of some odd places tomorrow."

She rolled her eyes. "Which reminds me. You better get your ass out of bed. You've got Chex Mix to clean up off the floor."

"It's fine. Henry will get it."

"Oh my God, Henry! He probably ate the whole bag!" *Jess leaped up, tossing on Todd's T-shirt, racing downstairs.*

The lazy dog hadn't even budged. The Chex Mix still coated the floor.

Jess grinned, shaking her head. Her life was ridiculous, childish, and just the way she liked it.

Figuring the mess could wait another day, she turned, went back up the steps, and snuggled right back in to the place where she belonged.

***

THREE WEEKS AGO

The Yahtzee-playing, Chex Mix-spilling day had only been three weeks ago. Sitting here now, though, her hands and toes frozen, survival only a tiny morsel of possibility, the night seemed like a different lifetime. She barely recognized the people in her memories, the carefree couple laughing about Chex Mix crumbs.

She'd give anything to feel those crumbs in her hair right

now, to chase Todd upstairs to their warm bed.

She shook so hard she could barely breathe. The inky night wrapped itself around the truck, hammering it with even colder temperatures. Jessica had thought she'd been cold before; now it was a different kind of cold, the night air drenching them in an iciness more intense. Her chest ached with the burn of the icy air. She turned her head to look at Todd.

He also shook brutally. They'd fallen into a hazy, drunken sleep, their fading body condition helping them slip into a slumber for far too long.

We need to start the truck, she thought. Her lips hurt too much to spit out the words. Her arms ached, but she leaned toward the keys, readjusting herself painstakingly so she could flick her wrist and start the truck.

She turned the key and the truck sputtered and choked.

Nothing.

It was fine. It had done this before. She tried again.

Nothing.

"Come on," she yelled, and Todd jumped.

She tried again.

Mercifully, it coughed to life.

She eased back to her spot, holding her hands to warm them.

A few minutes of warmth caressed her hands, her soul. Her breathing came a little bit easier.

And then it happened.

Chapter Nineteen

"No," she whimpered, turning to Todd. "No."

With the simple word, she pleaded with the universe, begged it with all she had. She didn't want to believe it, even though the harsh truth slapped her in the face. They'd lost so much hope. They'd dealt with hunger, unwavering cold, and the constant fear of the unknown. They'd held on, though, clinging to a small relic of hope, a small vision of tomorrow.

Now, though, she knew it was completely over for them. The visions of tomorrow, the remnants of possibility, had cracked. They were finished.

She inched toward the ignition, crossing her gloved fingers before turning the engine off and back on.

Nothing.

The truck was dead. The gas was gone.

Their lives were balancing precariously in the hands of time.

Tears slid down her face, stinging her eyes. Todd, still cold, still wrestling the demons of his hurt leg, reached out a wavering hand to her. He touched her shoulder, and she sank back into him, huddled in a fetal position. She rocked, tears soaking his jacket.

"We're done."

He ran a shaking hand through her hair, stroked her cheek before his icy lips found hers. He was silent, though, the kiss more like a kiss of death than a kiss of reassurance. He didn't tell her she was wrong. He didn't shake his head. He just squeezed her close.

The tears slowly subsided. She had no choice. She couldn't cry herself to death.

She wrapped up near Todd's beard, nestled against his neck. Despite the bitterness of the situation and the temperature, she felt her heart soften.

She felt love between them. This man loved her, would love her until her final breath, even if it was coming soon. She could at least take comfort in that, find warmth in that.

She mourned in silence for a while, thinking about how sad their story was. Todd held her close, also silent, perhaps mourning in his own way. The moments ticked by, her mind wrapping around the nonsensical situation, around the shock of it. Her mind toyed with the notion, with the finality that it all ended like this. There were no more pages in their book, no more memories to make. They would end it all here, frozen, frightened, and slipping away.

Neither said anything, choked by feelings of hopelessness and defeat. They clung to each other, the only beacons of sanity and humanity left in the truck. The truck was no longer a semi-haven in the midst of tragedy; instead, it had become a trap, a tomb, a curse. The only beacons left were their beating hearts, their memories, and their connection.

Time passed, probably a lot of time. Finally, he broke the silence, one word disconcertingly slipping off his tongue. That one word, though, held enough power to rebound off her heart and bounce her from her forlorn coffin of thoughts.

"Go."

The word drifted between them for a while. Her hands, her mind, her heart were too numb to accept it.

"What?"

"Y-you need to go." Each word was a chore as the temperature continued to drop. "I-in m-m-orning."

"N-no."

She fought the words, wanted to bash them off the snow-covered windshield. How could she even think of leaving Todd? They were in this together. She'd promised herself that. They would face whatever came with certainty.

Still, the thought crept up on her. Maybe he was right. Maybe she was being foolish. She could save them. She could do it. The scrappy girl who'd survived all of those foster homes, who'd been bullied and beaten up, she still existed in there somewhere. She could do this. She could be strong, could bear the weight of this burden for the both of them. She could save Todd, could save them.

She didn't want to leave him, afraid to think of what could happen.

But the thought of what could happen sitting here scared

her too.

She settled in with Todd, moving as close as she could without twisting him or his leg. She sidled up against his cheek, skin to skin, feeling his breath on her as she wrapped herself around him. Tears glided down her cheek, chilling her even more, but she didn't care.

She didn't want the thought to sneak in, so she fought it down like she fought down rising bile on a night of drinking. She didn't want to think the words she chanted in her mind, but she couldn't help it.

What if this is our last night together? What if this is it? The words echoed within her, dancing around her heart, teasing her with anxiety.

She squeezed him tighter, not ever wanting to let go, not ever wanting to think about this being goodbye. She was pissed she had to face this. Hadn't she endured enough trials in her life? Hadn't she survived enough hurdles? Where was the justice in the world?

She realized now, though, that justice didn't exist, something she should've learned a long time ago. Something she had learned but forgotten, love clouding her reality goggles.

The reality goggles were back now. She had to survive another night here. Todd slipped further away with every passing moment. And the next morning, she would leave him, trek out into the unknown, and try to make it back in time.

But if she didn't, this would be her last night with the man who had opened up her entire world, who had changed her, who made her the Jessica she was today. Even if she survived physically, Jessica Kling would be essentially pronounced dead, her soul and heart buried six feet under, snow caked right on top, the icy shell of the woman left to roam the earth in search of peace.

***

The night was a conglomeration of shivers, snot, tears, rumbling stomachs, and worries. They slept on and off, huddled together, trying to ignore the fact that the cold rotted their ability to think. They tried to keep their fingers and toes moving, to fight the aching cold settling into their bones, a sure sign of frostbite or hypothermia. It was the most miserable night so far, the reprieve from the truck's heater no longer an option. Suddenly, the night before seemed like a distant, royal memory of a cushy time.

They survived, though, few words between them. There was nothing to say, and they were too tired to say anything anyway. They spoke instead in the wordless touches, the soothing caresses, the proximity of their breath. They said so much without saying a word, their hearts knowing each other so intimately that no words were necessary.

Still, the physical conditions were not conducive to romance, and even Todd's love for her didn't make it any less cold. By morning, they were a stammering, freezing mess.

"I-I-I g-g-g-et h-h-e-e-e-lp," she stuttered, trembling. Todd gave her a wistful look before nodding.

"L-love." It was one word, but it brought tears to her eyes. The single word summarized them, who they were, and what they were.

They were simply love.

She got her head back in the game, thinking about the trip, about ways to make it more likely she would survive. She took his pocket knife, deciding to cut more of the seat for insulation. It was a much harder task, her hands numbing in the cold. Without relief from the heater all night, the brutal cold had settled deep within her. She took her time, focusing all of her energy on the task. She managed to fight through the pain as she moved her aching hands. It took a long, long time, but she managed to crudely cut some more insulation from the truck seat without cutting open her hand, tucking it into her jacket to insulate her. She also tucked some into Todd's welding boots, hoping to protect the loose-fitting boots from taking in too much snow.

She was inadequately prepared, she knew. They didn't have any food for her to take. It was going to be a treacherously long walk.

But she had to try. They were desperate.

She inhaled, knowing the moment she dreaded had arrived. She needed to say goodbye.

Tears streamed down her face, stinging her cheeks. Her chest ached with heaviness, as if it were literally splitting into a million little pieces.

Todd reached up to wipe her tears away, his hand unsteady.

She didn't say "I love you," didn't offer a teary, beautiful monologue. Instead, she leaned in and kissed him for what could be the last time. They clung to each other's frozen lips, savoring the emotion passing between them. Words weren't needed. Their connection was palpable from across a room, from a phone conversation, or from a frozen kiss in a deadly situation.

She gave him one last look, handed him the painkillers, and rolled down the window. She didn't look back as she plummeted from the window, didn't turn around for fear of losing her resolve.

The snow fell lightly, but the worse problem was the wind. It blew against her, pounding her body, making any movement difficult. Grayness drenched the day. She glanced up toward the embankment, the road still covered.

She'd considered the best route. The road seemed like an ingenious choice, the possibility of a car passing making it seem like a no-brainer. However, climbing the mountainous road would be difficult, energy-draining, and counterproductive if no cars passed her—which was extremely likely. The snowplow from the day before was probably just a fluke, as it had been the first one they'd heard during their ordeal. The chances of seeing another one or another vehicle at all seemed slim.

The better path, although a more frightening one, would be down through the woods. If she walked far enough, by her estimation, she could reach a tiny town about twenty miles away. She worried about getting there by nightfall. She worried about not having a map. In all likelihood, she would die out there, alone, in the wilderness.

She brushed the fear off. She had to try.

Choosing a branch as a walking stick, she began her journey, marching through the snow, sweat already rolling on her face despite the cold. She panted and stumbled, the weakness in her legs making the journey impossible.

She walked on, slogging through snow and wind. She kept fighting, knowing Todd depended on her.

Todd.

The man who had saved her from her demons, herself, a life of loneliness. The man who strutted into her life in a pair of jeans and stole her heart over some mac and cheese.

She paused, her lips quivering, her fingers numb. She looked in front of her, snow whipping in her face. The silence drowned her. Still, a beauty existed here, all alone, in the peace of the wilderness, the only thing to keep her company barren tree branches and snow. Snow coated the trees, the ground, in a cloak of quietude, of icy bereavement. She turned around, but the truck had vanished out of sight already, the wilderness cloaking it. She'd made some progress, although not nearly enough. Still, she should keep going, keep trying. It felt hopeless, her aching body telling her to stop, to give up, but she knew she should keep trying. To keep trying was to at least give them a chance at making it out of this. At least she could say she tried.

Like a siren's song, the wilderness sang to her, urging her to keep going, to trudge deeper into its icy grasp. She'd come here to save them, to fight the impossible, to find a miracle. She listened, but her resolve wavered. Her steps slowed, and her body and mind got heavier.

She should keep going. She should tough it out.

But she didn't know if she wanted to. She paused, staring into the open expanse of the forest, the great unknown. She gaped at the trees, at the snow-covered ground, at the snow-filled sky. Her body, heart, and mind stilled. She listened to the silence and heard everything she needed. The silent, snowy wilderness spoke to her, gave her the answer.

The miracle wasn't here. It couldn't be. Because without Todd, there was no miracle.

She needed to go back to him. Suddenly, her shaking hands and chilled face were nothing compared to the throbbing of her empty heart. She ached for him, craved his touch.

From a survival perspective, it was suicide to go back, to give up now. To have marched this far for nothing was a waste of resources, energy, and time. From the standpoint of her heart, though, it was suicide to continue.

Whatever happened to them, she wanted it to happen to them as a couple, not as individuals. With clarity, she realized that, life or death, having his hand to hold mattered more than anything else. She wanted to live, wanted to survive against the odds.

She couldn't give up on Todd, give up what could be their final moments together, for an empty promise that would probably prove futile.

They would face the future together, whatever it held. They would, hand in hand, meander back into their lives of Netflix, Pizza Hut, and work. Or they would, hand in hand, roam into the great unknown, comforted by the fact that they were together.

She took one last glimpse at the forest, kissed its promises goodbye, and turned around, edging backward but also forward at the same time. She edged back to reclaim her heart, which she'd left in the truck in the snowdrift.

***

The hike back to the truck felt like forever. She hadn't realized how far she'd made it. Still, she knew she was doing the right thing.

Please God, she thought. *Please save us somehow.* She'd sworn off hope, told herself she'd given up. Yet, somewhere deep inside, a sliver of optimism still persisted, if only because of her desperate want to live.

She gritted her teeth, clenched her jaw, and fought back through the snow, her body growing colder by the second. She prayed she wasn't too late, prayed she'd find Todd still clinging to life.

Why had she left in the first place? She'd known when she stepped out of the truck she couldn't do it, couldn't leave him.

That was their promise to each other, the vow they'd clung to the most.

They would never leave each other.

She'd been left behind so many times in her life. The leaving left open wounds all through her. She was a patched-up rag doll, torn at the seams from the ins and outs in her life.

Todd had sewn her back together, had helped her realize love could last, helped her see not every man walked out.

Even at her worst, he'd clung to her, had refused to leave, even when she'd violently tried to get rid of him.

***

Her head throbbing, she plucked another shiny pill from

the bottle, shoving it down her throat with precision before plodding back to her sanctuary.

Lately, though, the down comforter she'd been huddled in felt like a straitjacket, the bedroom a maximum-security jail cell.

Her own mind was her warden, laying claim to every aspect of the Jessica she used to be.

Bailey's death had shredded that woman. All of the bruises from the Brownsons, all of the ugly memories were nothing compared to the scars she carried on her heart, the deep lacerations still oozing sorrow within.

It had been a month, but for Jessica, it was still September 2 every single day. Every day, she got on the carousel of memories and whirred through them over and over again. The van... the decision... the death.

It was her fault. Her stupid choices had led to her baby's death. She'd murdered her child.

Friends, coworkers, neighbors had tried to obliterate the pain with casseroles and flowers. Their sweet words of comfort were just daily dirges, stabbing her with every single note. There was no forward or backward, no up or down. There was just this murky region in her bed, in her mind, and in her heart of hell on Earth, of sadness unbearable. Her baby had died.

She wanted to be dead too.

Todd had been trying to yank her from the pit of sorrow. Concern bubbled in his eyes, lapped against her with his soothing words, his embraces, his expressed fears.

He'd begged her to see a therapist, asked if she thought about hurting herself. She'd overheard his hushed words with his mom on the phone, wondering if he should have her committed.

She hated what she was doing to him. He'd lost his baby too. He shouldn't have to shoulder all of this alone, shouldn't have to worry about losing his wife.

Her pain drowned him along with her. She was forcing his head underwater with her, tying an anvil to his foot and letting him slowly sink. It wasn't fair. Still, as much as she told herself she needed to snap out of it, needed to help support Todd, she couldn't.

Todd came into the room then, a cup of tea in his hand, his familiar black beanie on his head. He wordlessly placed the cup on the nightstand beside their wedding picture, walked around the bed, and climbed under the covers with her. He'd taken another day off work, another day to babysit her.

She didn't move a muscle, her gaze locked on the wall straight across from the bed—the empty, plain blue wall that had become her constant companion these days. It didn't ask questions, didn't tell her it was going to be okay.

"Jess," Todd started, reaching for her hand. She pulled away, tears falling again. "Baby, listen. I'm hurting too. What can I do to help? You need to let me help you."

She breathed through the crackling pain in her chest, still staring ahead.

"You can leave." She barely recognized her own voice, the scratchiness evidence of her muteness.

"Honey, don't be like this. Don't push me away."

"I said you need to leave." Her words were more forceful that time.

He inhaled. She could see from her peripheral vision that he was fixing his beanie, a nervous habit familiar to her.

"Look, I'll be in the living room." He started to move.

"I mean leave for good. Leave me."

He froze, his leg midway out of bed.

"What are you saying?"

She finally turned to him, the pain on his face suffocating her. She couldn't do this to him anymore.

"You need to leave me. You need to move on. I'm never going to be the woman you married again. I can't live with this. But I really can't live with ruining your life too. I've already hurt her. I can't hurt you too."

"Jess, stop. I know you're hurting, but this is crazy. You're not hurting me. It's killing me seeing you like this knowing nothing I do can make it better. I wish I could help you get through this. But I'm not leaving, no matter what. No matter how long it takes, no matter how long until you can let me in again, I'll be standing right here."

She cried harder. "I can't stop feeling like this, and I don't think I ever will be better. I can't watch you sitting by, throwing your life away on me."

Tears were slipping down his face too. She'd never seen him cry before Bailey's death. Todd was always the stoic man, the hard, steadfast man. Now the pain ripped him at the seams, too, and his tears were always close by.

"You listen to me. I love you, Jessica. I've loved you since the first day we ate mac and cheese at the diner. I loved you through all of our stupid fights over cereal boxes in the pantry and taking the garbage out. I loved you when you were puking

your guts out from too much drinking to the night you told me you were pregnant. And I loved you when we lost our baby girl. I love you now. My love is not going away. Me leaving would never change that. You have my entire heart. And even if you're struggling, which we both are, even if you're falling apart, I love you. I want to be with you. I want to be here for you. Let me be here for you, baby. Because I'm not leaving. I'm never leaving you, you hear me? I'm never leaving."

He leaned in, grabbing her face in his hands, planting a sweet kiss on her lips. He pulled back gently, leaning his forehead against hers. She sobbed into him, grabbing ahold of his arms, feeling herself finally giving in, finally letting herself lean on him.

They held each other that afternoon for hours, crying, mourning, wallowing with each other in pain. Having Todd by her side didn't lessen the pain, didn't make it any more bearable. Still, having him there reminded her she could do this, that she could breathe. He made her feel like she could breathe again, if only enough to survive.

The next day wasn't any easier. The next months weren't easier. In fact, things just got worse, eventually landing her in the mental ward for a while.

But she survived. After hitting rock bottom for a month, she started seeing a therapist regularly, started getting help. As time passed, the pain didn't dissipate completely, but it dulled to the point she could start functioning again. She started finding herself again, started finding a life without Bailey.

Most of all, though, she realized no matter what, she needed him. They needed each other.

He'd broken through with those words, the words she hadn't even realized she needed to hear.

He would never leave her. So many had left her before, but not Todd. Todd would never leave.

***

Her legs were leaden by the time she reached the familiar, rusty tan color of the truck. She practically threw herself against it, panting from exertion, happy to at least see this familiar sight. She knocked on the door, waiting for Todd to roll down the window that he'd rolled up after she'd left.

There was a long pause, one which grappled her heart with fear.

"Todd?" she asked, her voice unfamiliar even to her, its lack of use giving it an odd, scratchy quality.

She knocked on the window, her gloved hand pounding. She peered in, could make out Todd's shape leaning toward the window, until finally it started to go down. When it was down enough, she precariously lifted herself through the window. It took every ounce of energy she had left to propel herself into the cab, Todd grabbing her arm and tugging her in.

"W-what are y-you d-doing?" he stuttered, his eyes filled with complete confusion. He looked drained. Perhaps it was just because she'd been away from him for a while, or perhaps it was her imagination, but he looked worse than a few hours ago. He looked like he was fading.

Jessica settled into her seat, brushing off snow, rubbing her hands as she snuggled into him to warm up.

"I-I'll n-n-e-e-v-ver l-leave y-you," she stammered, repeating the familiar words.

Despite the predicament, despite what her return meant, he squeezed her arm. He knew what she meant. He got it.

No matter what happened, they'd face it together. They'd trudge into the uncertain—or perhaps more certain—future together. They'd be there for each other, not making the descent into death easier or less painful, but making it manageable because they were together. They'd remind each other to breathe until they couldn't anymore.

Then, two hearts, two minds, two souls, they'd exit life the way they'd lived it—together.

She still feared death. She wasn't ready to make her grand exit, to leave this world behind. She still had so much to do, so many loose ends, so many regrets. She hated that this had come at such a shocking time, at such an unexpected moment.

Nonetheless, sitting back in the truck with Todd, she felt a sense of peace too. She may have given up. She hadn't saved them, hadn't really tried. But she had realized what mattered most.

It was their love, their connection.

It was Todd. She would give up her life for him. She would give up the hope of survival if it meant she would be in his arms, would go into the great unknown with him by her side.

She'd given up hope for what mattered the most to her— love.

Settling back into him, she drifted into the freezing, murky world of her dreams.

Chapter Twenty

An unfamiliar sound startled her. She peeled her eyelids open, her heart beating fast as the sound got closer. Their icy breath came in plumes in the truck cab. Her toes and fingers ached and throbbed, as did her head. She couldn't wrap her head around what she heard.

Todd fluttered his eyes, stirring at the sound as well. It kept getting louder, kept getting closer. It was an odd sound, something she hadn't heard yet during their ordeal.

"Heli—" Todd said before sputtering into a coughing fit.

Her brain searched for the answer. *Heli... heli... what was it?*

"H-h-eli…," she started, but her voice cracked. *Helicopter,* she said in her mind. It was a helicopter.

Someone was looking for them. Todd's mom must have contacted the authorities. They'd pieced it together. They were looking for them.

Despite her shaking body, she wanted to leap for joy. She found the hope she'd thought had left, found the remnants of possibility she'd abandoned.

Someone was looking for them. They could survive after all.

She scrambled toward the window, her movements jerky and uncontrollable. Her hands and feet wouldn't obey her brain's directions. Her movements were tedious and painful. She was frustrated. She needed to get out there, to make sure they saw her.

The sound of the whirring helicopter started to soften, and she panicked. They'd left. They'd missed their chance. What if they hadn't seen them?

She wouldn't give up, though. Not now. She kept working toward the window, her hands moving despite their deteriorating condition. She willed them to move faster, and by some miracle, they seemed to obey.

She got the window down and managed to get herself to the window. She sat on the ledge, hanging on, her eyes scanning the sky. The helicopter couldn't be heard anymore. It was gone.

"I-itt-ll c-c-ome b-b-a-c-ck-k," Todd pronounced, warming his hands by rubbing them together. Despite the freezing temperatures and his frailty, a familiar hope clung to his face too. Some of the color seemed to come back, the possibility of survival warming him from the inside out.

She nodded, sitting perched on the window, waiting for the sound. She needed to be ready when it came back. She needed to wave them down.

She glanced to her right, the snow piled all around her. They had gotten a few more inches that day, but the snow wasn't falling anymore. Visibility had improved. Looking near the barren road, she saw a tiny speck of red. Squinting, she placed the speck in her mind.

The scarf. It remained in its spot. Snow had buried it, but

it had remained.

Her mind, still foggy from cold and exhaustion, curled itself around the idea. If she could get the scarf out, if she could wave it, maybe the helicopter would see the bright red against the snow. It was a long shot, probably didn't even make logical sense. Nonetheless, to her, it was the best she had. Without a way to start a fire or a smoke signal, it was all she could cling to.

Before she could think, she carefully turned around, propelling herself back into the chilling snow. It bit into her legs, still as shocking as ever. She trudged forward, though, driving herself through the snow drifts, one mission in mind.

Her legs hurt, and she tripped quite a few times. Each time she fell, she picked herself back up, her numb body no match for her determined mind. She plodded forward, each step like running a marathon, until she reached it.

Stooping to her hands and knees, she rooted in the snow, unearthing the symbol of her hope from just a few days back. Then this scarf had been a silly hope, a prayer really, a guiding light for her. It had been a vision for the future, a promise they'd make it out.

Now the scarf was buried, only a few threads still palpable.

Still, there were a few threads of optimism.

She pulled it out from its icy casket, snow coated on the beautiful red fabric. She brushed it off as best as she could, which wasn't really effective. The scarf, now a frozen block of red fabric, felt promising between her hands. She eyed it, running her hands over it. She shook it a bit, trying to clear away the snow and return the scarf to its former softness. Then she stood, a single speck in the middle of an icy sea, waiting, wondering how long until salvation would come.

She stood, shivering, her cheeks slapped with the freezing air that had become a familiar foe. The scarf waited between her hands, a sad, single hope from a frantic woman.

She stood like a martyr awaiting reckoning, like a lost child awaiting the return of a parent. She waited, her eyes on the sky, her ears begging for the echoing sound of safety, for the familiar hymn of rescue. Her lips murmured prayer after prayer, her hands outstretched, holding the scarf like a divine sacrifice to the universe.

The sound, though, did not come. The sight of redemption did not fill the sky. Her arms grew tired with the weight of the fake talisman, the relic of hope now shattered.

She stood, not willing to believe it was all for naught. It had been tough to accept the inevitability of their death, of the fact that help wasn't coming. Accepting failure now, though, when they'd been able to physically witness the possibility of rescue, of safety, was cataclysmic. To taste a possibility for victory, to be lifted from the utter pit of hopelessness back into the grasp of hope, only to be dropped back down again— it was undeterminably catastrophic. It was the blackest of blackness, the most depraved sadness, the most excruciating destruction.

It was death itself.

She stood until she heard Todd crying her name into the breeze, a prayer much like her own prayer for safety. Even then, she stood a moment longer, not quite ready to give in, not quite ready to acknowledge what must be acknowledged yet again.

When all was clearly lost and darkness descended, she let out a guttural sound from the pit of her wrecked soul. She screamed for the inequity of life, for the lost chance, for the hope no longer within their reach.

She tossed the scarf, still frozen and solid, to the ground, tamping it into what now seemed to be wretched snow. She kicked it, her overexerted body offering a weak assault at best on the object.

When she'd finished her frustrations, when she'd kicked her anger out, she headed back to the truck, one foot lumbering in front of the other like she'd done so many times now. Her feet slid through the snow on the way back, gliding a path as if she were on her own funeral march.

In many ways, she was.

She catapulted herself through the window, swearing it would be the last time. She said goodbye to the freezing air, the unforgiving wilderness, and took her feet off the ground for what she knew would be the last.

She rolled up the window, centimeter by aching centimeter, and leaned back against the seat, her despondency so deep she couldn't even muster a single tear.

Todd said nothing, his face probably matching the emotions on her own.

They sat in silence yet again, her eyes boring holes into the dash as frustration and turmoil bubbled within her chest. Slowly, she turned her head toward Todd, hoping to find some solace in his face, some comfort in him.

Instead, a tear dripped down his cheek, and she knew he felt exactly the same thing she did.

Lost again.

Someone was looking for them. But someone hadn't found them. They'd missed their chance. Their lucky numbers weren't called, and the game was moving on.

There was nothing to do now but slip into oblivion and wait for the end to come.

Chapter Twenty-One

The all-too-familiar hush deafened them, taunting them yet again. Brushing the snow haphazardly off, kicking the packed snow from her feet, she reclaimed her spot in the cab, repossessed her final resting place in her mind. She stared aimlessly forward, her gaze dancing on the windshield, caked with snow. It didn't matter. She didn't want to look outside anyway, didn't want to see the bleakness slammed in her face. She'd rather sit here, numbed physically and mentally.

"Th-th-ey'll c-c-ome b-b-b-ba-ck-ck," Todd stammered.

Jess simply shook her head slowly, forlornly, not even able to look at him as tears of disappointment streaked down her cheeks.

He carefully reached for her hand, still sopping wet from snow. He brought it painfully to his hands, blew on it, and then kissed it. She turned to him, sadness still drowning her.

"It-t-t's d-d-one," she said, an air of finality despite her stammering.

He said nothing, staring into her eyes. He gently pulled her over to him, and she gave in, leaning into his chest. His beard scratched against her cheek, but she didn't care. She didn't care anymore at all. *It was done.* She'd been a fool to think they could survive this. She'd been an idiot to put so much effort into trying.

The cab of the truck grew incrementally darker as they faded into another night.

The last night, she told herself. They couldn't possibly survive any longer. This would be the night, the final night they had together before heading into the great unknown.

She wasn't ready, still mourned for their life they had yet to live. Still, as her body ached from the cold, as her stomach growled, the release of death seemed somewhat welcoming. She had faith. She thought death couldn't possibly bring about anything worse than what they'd experienced here. The thought of closing her eyes, of drifting away, welcomed her. The hell would be over.

Leaning into Todd, who shuddered with cold, she first thought she'd imagined it. Then, however, she readjusted herself, and his lips almost imperceptibly moved against her cheek.

The words were broken and stuttered. They were barely audible. Still, in her mind, the music played on, swirling around her, gripping at her heart and making her breathe a little slower.

Todd, despite his pain and cold, sang their song, their wedding song and, for a second time in her mind, Jess danced with Todd. This time, though, they danced in a reception hall filled with loved ones, his tux scratchy against her cheek. They danced in her memories, the love reverberating between them made more real by the love she still felt for him.

Chapter Twenty-Two

NIGHT FOUR

This wasn't how it was supposed to be. This wasn't where their story was supposed to end. There was so much left to do, so much left unfinished. She didn't want the question mark filled in with starvation or dehydration or pneumonia or hypothermia or whatever else they could fill in the blank. These days, the choices were plentiful.

She wanted to leave her cause of death a question. She wanted to leave the mystery for another day.

"T-t-odd?" she stammered, her voice cracking, her words almost inaudible.

He didn't respond.

"T-t-odd," she said again, this time moving her arm to touch him, the movement also difficult.

A groan escaped from his lips.

"Todd, you can't... sleep.... Not now."

Silence. Bone-chilling silence.

And then, finally, a mumble, words crackling. "I'm...h-here. I'm s-still—"

The words, though, weren't reassuring. They weren't the words of a man reaffirming his hold on life, his will to survive.

She wanted to cry, but she couldn't. She was too hungry, too thirsty, too tired, and too cold to cry. She'd done enough of that. She kept staring at him, the man who had been her rock. The man she wanted to grow old with. The man she'd pledged her life to.

Was this really how it would all end?

"D-do y-o-u... w-w-h-h-e-en... f-f-ell... l-l-o-ove?" The words were broken. She didn't think he understood.

He didn't respond verbally, but he responded enough to tell her he did, that he would go there with her to this memory. He squeezed her hand, and she felt him go along with her to the moment that would define them, the moment when they realized their love was real.

***

Todd held the picnic basket with one hand, and his other hand held Jess's. Jess pulled her hand out of his momentarily to readjust her shorts. She felt a little self-conscious, her tank top and cutoffs showing off a little more than she usually would. She tried not to think about it, though, Todd's story about getting stuck in the deck railing as a child easing her away from her fears.

It had been two months since their mac and cheese date at the diner. It had been two months since the jeans-wearing man with a beard had stomped into her life and started wrestling with her heart. It had been two months since she'd felt an unfamiliar warmth creeping into her, seizing her, making her let down her guard.

In two months, they'd been exploring this thing between them, the emotions deepening with every coffee date, every take-out pizza, every trip to the movies.

She'd fought it at first, not ready to give in to him, not ready to let go of her heart. Not quite ready to trust him. Still, she had to admit that, every moment they were apart, he invaded her thoughts. She found herself counting the hours until she'd see him again, wondering if he'd pop by and surprise her with her favorite ice cream or an impromptu movie night. She'd found herself checking her phone for his number more frequently. She found herself looking forward to his animated stories, to the way he talked with his hands, to his hearty laugh.

She'd fallen for him, she realized as they waded through the hip-high grass toward the dock. She'd irrevocably fallen for him. It was more than love, which he'd confessed to her at the zoo a few weeks ago. It was a life-altering connection. It was a relationship growing deeper every moment.

It was serious.

Something about Todd Kling soothed her, made her feel like she could fall. For the first time in her life, an unidentifiable rationale told her if she fell, it wouldn't be too far because he'd be right there to catch her.

There were no guarantees, she knew. It had only been

two months. Still, in those two months together, Todd had made her laugh, made her feel safe, made her feel wanted. He hadn't pushed too hard. They'd kissed quite a few times, and they'd made it to second base, but that was it. He was okay with taking their time, which was just what she needed.

She'd met his parents and had found comfort in his homey childhood house and sweet family dynamic. She liked the way he kissed his mom on the cheek before they left and the way he looked at her with reverence. She liked that he had a solid, stable family foundation, unlike her.

It was so much more than his family, though. It was in the way he held doors for her, the way he laughed with her. It was in the way he wasn't afraid to go out and live life, to call her to go get tacos at eleven at night on a Wednesday or to splurge and get them front row tickets to a baseball game just because. He was a life liver, just like she wanted to be. He completed her.

"Man, it's gorgeous out, huh?" he said as he pulled her up on the boards of the dock, the water of the lake lapping against the shore. The sun beamed down on them with intensity, warming her skin and her cheeks.

"So we're at this point now? Where we talk about the weather?" she teased as she kicked off her flip-flops, feeling the scratchy wood beneath her bare feet.

He grinned at her. "Sorry. I didn't know weather was off-limits."

"I'm just being a jerk. You're right. It is beautiful. I've never been here."

He set the picnic basket down and led her to the edge of

the dock. They took a seat on the boards. In the distance, some kayakers glided across the water. Some kids jumped off the back of a small boat, their screams ricocheting off the wilderness. This dock, though, was empty except for them. It was their own little corner of the outdoors. She was happy to be sitting here with him.

"Really?"

She nodded. "Yeah. I didn't really get out much. The families I lived with either weren't into the outdoors or were too cheap to drive us out here even for the day."

He squeezed her hand. She'd already told him about her past, hadn't wanted to hide it. She'd always been upfront about her childhood, not embarrassed by it. It was a part of her, whether she liked it or not. She thought she owed it to herself to be honest about it, to not let it shame her.

Todd leaned in and kissed her hand, and electricity jolted through her. "I'm glad I get to be the one to bring you here," he said.

She smiled. "It's beautiful."

He let go of her hand for a second to reach into their basket. He pulled out two bottles of beer, handing her one.

She raised an eyebrow. "Getting me drinking already? It's only noon." Still, she took the bottle.

"It's like an unwritten rule. When you sit on the dock, you have to drink a beer. Besides, it's Saturday. Alcohol drinking rules don't apply on gorgeous Saturdays like this at the lake." He grabbed his bottle opener from his keyring and popped open both beers. They sipped on them.

She warmed from the sun, from the beauty of the moment,

from the alcohol, and mostly from him. Sitting there, taking in the sights of the lake and the feel of the breeze on her bare skin, she saw so much more than the scene before her. She saw a life of dock sitting, of beer drinking, of ambling through easy conversations with this man beside her. She saw a life of new experiences and easy laughter.

It scared her a little, if she was honest. Relationships and commitment had always been things to push aside, to shrug off in favor of building a life. She'd been burned too many times, had been hurt and broken down. She'd vowed to herself that she'd focus on herself, wouldn't lean on anyone. She'd be strong, independent, alone.

Leaning on Todd's shoulder, though, sharing the beauty of the moment, her soul sighed. It felt good to lean on someone, to share with someone, to just be with someone.

It felt good to be here with Todd.

She set down her beer, leaning in, the sun still gleaming. He turned, noticing the look in her eyes, and set down his beer too.

He went all in, just like she liked. He took her face gently in his hands, tilted his head, and took her lips in his. He kissed her sweetly but hungrily. He kissed her like it was his job, his mission, his passion in life. He kissed her like he'd known her for ten years and not just two months.

He kissed her as if she were meant for him.

In that moment, the lake still lapping, the kids still screaming in the distance, her heart gave in completely. That kiss, that picturesque scene sold it to her.

She was done guarding her heart. She was done holding back.

Two weeks, two months, two years—it didn't matter.

He was it for her. He softened her heart, showed her what real love was. He was the one to take her to the lake for the first time. He made her believe in a love of her own. He restored her faith in a relationship, in a union, in a family not marked by abuse and negligence.

He was, quite simply, the one.

When they pulled back gently, sweat beading on their foreheads from the heat of the day, she smiled. She kept her face close, just an inch apart from his.

"I love you," she whispered, the words dancing off her tongue into the breeze.

The words were an oath, a sworn vow from her heart to his. She loved him. She said it out loud, the three words she'd never actually said in her entire life. Now, sitting here on the dock, she knew without a doubt they were the truest words she could speak. She owned them and what they meant. She was ready to tell him she felt the same way. She was finally ready to tell him that what he'd told her two weeks ago in front of the jellyfish was exactly the way she felt too. More than that, she was ready to tell herself that it was okay to love him.

"I love you too. Forever. Always. Until my dying breath," he whispered back, and they kissed some more.

When they were completely love drunk from the kissing and confessions, they scooched their beers and the basket to the side and lay down on their backs beside each other, their feet dangling over the edge. Holding hands, they closed their eyes, the sounds of the lake lulling them into a state of serenity.

Eventually, they would make their way to the nearby

picnic table. They ate peanut butter sandwiches and some Oreos, talking about childhoods, dreams, and embarrassing moments. They talked about the present. They talked about the future.

Most of all, they basked in the easygoing nature of their love, of the fact that they knew without a doubt this was it for them. Their hearts were sealed together, promised to each other over some now-warm beer at the edge of a splintery dock.

Their vow that day had been stronger than any church ceremony or exchange of rings.

On that crystal-clear hot day, they'd pledged to break down the walls of Jessica's heart, to promise forever to each other.

It was that day that Jess went from being the broken, guarded, tough girl who would do it all alone to the trusting girl who could lean on Todd without a doubt.

On the dock, they'd realized the mac and cheese at the diner had really, truly been the best thing around.

***

Finding strength she didn't know she had, the memory perhaps fortifying her, she whispered, "Until our dying breath."

Glancing over at the man who'd thawed her heart that beautiful Saturday at the lake, who had sent out a life preserver to catch her from the waves of mistrust, she saw a tear sliding down his cheek. "Until our dying breath," he said back, his words unwavering despite his chattering teeth.

Who would have thought it would end like this? It just can't end like this, she thought as she leaned a little closer, holding both of Todd's hands, wishing they could go back and lie on the dock a little while longer.

Chapter Twenty-Three

Jess no longer had the strength to move. Hours of darkness swirled around her as she fought against the cold. Her fight was, inarguably, half-hearted now. She knew deep within that this was it. They would be gone by morning or soon after.

No words passed between them now, the only sound their labored breathing, their chattering teeth. She was so cold she couldn't think, could barely will herself to breathe in and out, the iciness of the air burning her lungs with each breath. She sat huddled into Todd, his closeness the only reminder she wasn't alone. He was silent, too, slipping into oblivion with each passing moment.

They sat, both hands in each other's, clenched tightly from the cold. As much as she wasn't ready to go, she wanted the end to come, wanted a merciful finish line to this epically tragic saga. They'd given it their all. They'd hung on as long as they could. Now it was time for a reprieve.

She could tell from the way the dash looked that the night

was breaking. The sun would be coming up soon. Against all odds, they'd survived another night—almost. There was no miracle to be celebrated here, though.

They were so close to the end.

She faded between the stupor of sleep and the pain of consciousness, her eyes barely staying open, the sagging lids tempting her to just give in to the unconsciousness of dreamworld. But she knew if she closed her eyes, she'd probably never wake up again. The finality of it, the goodbye element of it, disturbed her, despite her dazed mind.

She tried to focus her eyes on a spot on the windshield but couldn't. The pain, the fatigue, the weakness taunted her. It was too much.

Suddenly, a light eased into her field of vision. It was soft and eerie, radiating a palpable warmth. It came from outside but then, right before her eyes, it glowed inside the truck. A ball of light danced around the truck, spreading its balminess, its comfort.

"T-t-o-o-d-d," she whispered between cracked lips. He didn't stir. She wondered if he saw it, too, if he felt its effects.

The pain and anguish seemed to vacate her body. Her only link to the truck, to the cold, were Todd's hands clenched around hers, his icy fingers in hers. Soon even that faded away.

She warmed, head to toe. She wriggled her toes, the beauty of the feeling making her want to laugh. It felt so good to be warm again, to not be cracking under the coldness. She breathed in and out, the warmth radiating through her veins.

In front of her, in a hazy vision of light, he stood.

"T-t-o-o-d-d," she said again. She knew his hands, still

cold, were in hers, knew this with every rational bone in her body. But against all explanation, he stood there, right in front of her. He wore shorts and a sleeveless shirt, the one he wore that day on the dock. His eyes sparkled at her, and he extended a hand toward her.

"Come on, baby. It's time to go," he said to her.

She was so bewildered. Her head hurt, pounded against her skull. How did he change clothes? How was he standing in front of her, in the light? He'd been right beside her, holding her hand. What was happening?

The more she questioned it, though, the more confused she got. Her head pounded some more, her breathing intensifying.

"Hey, breathe, baby. It's okay. It's all going to be okay. Come on. Come with me," Todd said.

She still hesitated, a weird sensation creeping into her chest. Still, he was bathed in sunlight, basking in its glow. It was Todd all right, his blue eyes, his rugged beard, his welcoming grin. He extended a hand to her, and she reached out slowly. She wanted to take it. Looking into his eyes, she saw what she'd always seen, since the first day at the wedding—trust. She saw trust.

She reached out and touched his hand. It was warm, just like it'd always been. The rest of her doubts slipped away. Now that she'd taken his hand, she could see beyond him. They were at the lake, standing on the very dock where she'd first confessed her love.

"Come on, Jess. Come on."

He languidly strolled down the dock, and Jess followed. Looking down, her feet were still shoved in the winter boots.

She thought about taking them off but didn't want to ruin the moment.

As they strolled down the dock, her fogginess, her pounding head softened. It felt good to be in the sunshine, to have her hand in Todd's, to have him leading the way.

They got to the end of the dock, and her heart started pounding. It couldn't be. There was no way... but she was.

She *was* there. Jess would recognize her face anywhere, even if she'd never seen it in real life.

Standing in a pink tank top and an even pinker tutu, gorgeous black curls around her face, the girl stood at the edge of the dock. Wordlessly, she stared back at Jess with blue eyes. Jess crumpled to the dock, the power of the emotion overpowering her.

Bailey. In her heart, Jess knew it was her. The face, the features, the feeling radiating within Jess's chest.

Her little girl stood in front of her. She twirled once for Jess. She held a yellow rose, which had always been Jess's favorite.

"Is that...?" she asked in disbelief, processing but still hesitant to believe. Her heart ached, her heart smiled. It had to be. She'd know the face, even though she'd never seen it at this age. She just knew.

"Yes, baby."

Tears formed in Jess's eyes, but they were happy tears. She stooped down, her hands covering her face, gathering her composure.

"Mommy," the little voice said, and Jess thought she'd fall into the lake right there. The word she'd never gotten to hear, the word she'd waited forever to hear.

The little girl started walking toward her. Jess outstretched her arms. She knew if she was here, it could only mean one thing. Jess didn't care, though. Suddenly, the snowstorm, the entrapment, the pain all faded away. She was here with her little girl. Nothing mattered anymore. They would all be together.

As Bailey walked carefully onto the dock, the yellow rose stretched toward her, something yanked Jess's hand. Something shook her aggressively.

She turned, but Todd still stood beside her, a confused look on his face as well.

The force of the shaking caused her to close her eyes.

A surge of cold air slapped against her face, the warmth of the summer sun gone.

"Hello?" a voice said. It was a husky voice, not Todd's, no one she recognized.

"Hello?" the voice repeated. More gruff shaking, more cold, her head pounding again. Jess turned, trying to assess the situation. She saw the familiar, icy windshield, the dashboard. A light shone into the cab. Her hands were still locked in Todd's icy fingers.

She turned her head to the left just a hair and saw what appeared to be a man leaning over her.

She was even more confused now and, in reality, even more hurt. Her little girl had been ripped away again. She'd been there, right there. Jess had almost touched her, had almost gotten to hold her in her arms.

She fought back the tears as she formed the word on her

lips, a whisper coming off her lips again.

"B-b-b-a-a-a-i-i-l-e-e-y," she said, and then her eyes closed again.

Chapter Twenty-Four

SAM

"Dammit," he screamed, his fist hitting the dashboard. He knew he'd messed up. He knew the sign was wrong and the tree line didn't look right. He knew nothing looked familiar. He should've trusted his gut, should've turned around.

It had already been a hellishly long shift. He was going on hour eleven, the subsequent snowstorms over the last few days forcing mandatory overtime to kick in. He was exhausted, he was cold, and he wanted nothing more than to get in his shower, climb into bed with Liz, and snuggle up to his wife.

She'd probably be up already by the time he got home, in all reality. She'd be scampering about the house, taking care of little Ellen and getting her ready for school. He hated this third trick shift right now. Still, being bottom man meant you got the shitty shifts, like driving this godforsaken snowplow in the middle of nowhere in the middle of the night.

And it didn't help when you took a wrong turn, ending up in the absolute middle of nowhere.

He grabbed his cell phone from the seat beside him, hoping to cue up the GPS and get back on track so he could get the job done, get home, and get to bed.

Nothing. No signal in this backwoods region.

Figured.

Pulling out the two-way radio on the dash, he radioed back to the barracks. "Uh, yeah, this is Sam. Took a wrong turn. Going to be running a few late getting back. Over."

A few minutes went by. "Roger," a voice replied. At least they knew he was on his way.

He stamped down on the gas, climbing the winding mountain road. Great. Now he'd be stuck at the top of some stupid mountain, knowing his luck. He thought about stopping the snowplow, turning around in the middle of the road, and just heading back down. It wasn't like there was any traffic up here anyway. It would be a while until he could get the thing turned around, but he could do it. It would be better than driving up the mountain.

"Screw it," he said, figuring he might as well keep the course now. It would be even longer until he got home if he accidentally drove off the side of the road and buried this thing in the snow. It would potentially be an eternity until he got to his shower then.

He turned up the country song blaring over the speakers. He'd brought a couple of CDs to keep him company. This one was the one Liz had made for him for their anniversary. It was filled with "their" songs. It made him smile a little. He ran a hand over his stubbly jaw, belting out a few notes.

He continued up the road, into the middle of nowhere. The levels of snow continued to increase as he climbed. He pitied anyone who'd tried to pass over this road within the past few days. He was lucky he drove a plow truck, or he'd probably be stuck.

Tapping along to the song on the steering wheel, he glanced to his left. The darkness of the night slowly faded, the hazy gray of predawn letting him see into the abyss. Not that there was much to see. Tree after tree, empty embankment after embankment, pile of snow after pile of snow.

As he veered up the mountain around a sharp turn, though, he thought his eyes played a trick on him. His headlights had lit up an area under the trees, far from the road. He could've sworn….

No, impossible. It was just his lack of sleep, his lack of caffeine, and his bad mood playing tricks on him.

Surely it couldn't have been. Even if it had been, it wasn't like anyone would be down there. They'd be long gone. It was stupid.

He slowed the speed of the truck, though, his thoughts bombarding against his head. What-ifs and curiosity got the better of him. He slowed, turned around the next curve, and found a small pull-off. He put the truck in Park, sighed, told himself he was crazy and opened his door.

The wind had died down, but the bitter cold ravaged his skin. The grayness was uncanny, along with the silence of the solitude. He grabbed a flashlight from behind his seat, lit up the path in front of him, and headed back down the road.

He must have a death wish, being out here alone, in the cold. He'd officially lost it. He wouldn't even tell Liz about this. She'd have him committed.

Nevertheless, something nagged at him, played on him. He zipped up his coat a little tighter, his steel-toed boots tromping down the road. He crossed the pavement to the other side of the road, shining his flashlight in the area he thought he'd seen something.

His beam of light landed on a large object underneath a group of trees.

"Holy fuck," he shouted, shock freezing him in place. He ran a hand over his head, warm underneath his trustworthy black hat.

Then, without thinking, he did what he knew he had to do.

He dashed down the embankment, his feet almost getting ahead of him as he ran through the snow, willing his feet to move faster.

He trudged through feet of snow, his jeans now soaked. He panted with the effort, as it was a good way down to the truck. In reality, he didn't know how he'd even seen it. It was pure luck he'd been glancing that way, had caught a hint of anything.

His feet felt like lead by the time he got to the truck, buried and covered in branches.

There were no signs of life other than what looked like a discarded red scarf tucked in some snow. It looked pretty rough. Maybe the people who'd been here had been rescued already, had walked out, or had just abandoned their vehicle. Surely no one could still be in there.

When he made his way to the door of the truck, though, he pounded on it just to be safe. He didn't want to take any chances there was still someone in there.

No one responded.

He pounded again.

Still nothing.

The truck was in terrible condition. He figured it would be better to play it safe, to make sure no one was in there. He'd come this far, so he may as well just finish it off, be sure.

He reached into his pocket for his key ring, happy he'd listened to Liz and put the tool on that he'd once thought was stupid. Now he grabbed his window punch and, with as much force as he could muster, stamped it against the window.

It shattered into millions of tiny fragments. He shined his

flashlight inside the cab.

The beam landed on two bodies.

"Oh my God," he whispered, his hand covering his mouth. They looked like they'd been dead for a while, neither moving. They were in terrible condition and had apparently been there for quite some time.

Moving into action quickly, Sam used a nearby twig to clear more glass away. He made sure there were no shards ready to puncture him before hoisting himself through the window, his feet dangling.

"Hello?" he said, reaching to shake the woman, who sat nearest to the window. "Hello?" he said, desperation creeping into his voice.

She stirred, slowly, almost invisibly. She had stirred, though. She was alive.

He shook her gently this time as her eyes fluttered. She squinted, her head turning toward him. She looked confused, gone, lost.

She did, after an arduously long time, manage to stutter one word.

Bailey.

"It's going to be okay, Bailey," he said, figuring it must've been her name. "Is he okay beside you?"

She squinted, still confused. She didn't seem to comprehend his question. He climbed in farther, being careful not to land on her. The banged-up truck was in awful condition. They'd apparently wrecked a few days ago. He leaned over her, though, knowing time was of the essence. He reached for the man beside Bailey, shaking his shoulder.

Nothing. He didn't move.

"Okay, listen," Sam said, knowing he needed to act fast. "Bailey, I'm going to be right back. I'm getting help. You hang in there."

"N-n-n-o-o-o," the woman croaked, her voice barely a whisper.

He patted her shoulder. Her black hair was matted in frozen clumps around her face.

She had the same hair his Liz had. He grew emotional but shrugged it off. He didn't have time for this right now.

He gave her a reassuring look, hoisted himself to the ground, and broke into a run through the tracks he previously made. He practically crawled up the embankment, stumbling and sliding. He finally made it to his truck, hoisting himself in. Out of breath, he grabbed his radio. "Sam to station. No joke. Emergency. Two stranded. One potentially dead but one alive. I need an ambulance and rescue crew stat."

"Roger. Tell us your location," a voice urgently responded.

Sam reported his location to the best of his ability. He begged them to hurry.

He stood outside his truck, stomping his feet, staring down the road at the place where a woman clung to life.

"Please be okay," he said out loud to himself. "Please make it."

When the ambulance, fire crew, and rescue unit came whirring up the road, Sam flagged them down, urging them toward the scene, trying to help in every way he could.

After an hour of work, of clearing pathways, of making the rescue, Bailey and the man beside her were off in an ambulance, off to the nearby hospital where, God willing, they'd survive.

They'd both survive.

It had been a long night. He still needed his shower.

But he was going home tonight a little bit more thankful, a little bit grateful for his life, for his shower, for the fact that he'd get to go home to his wife.

He was also thankful he'd taken the wrong turn.

Chapter Twenty-Five

JESS

She peeled her eyes open, a bright light blaring, her head pounding. She peeked around the area, taking inventory of the glaring white ceiling tiles, the beeping in her right ear, and the odd smell.

Then she noticed something strange.

She wasn't cold.

Wrapped in blankets and more blankets, she felt warm at last.

Am I dead? she wondered, the lights above combining with the white, confusing her mind.

"Mrs. Kling, can you hear me?" a voice beside her asked. She turned her head slowly to see a man in a white coat, a stethoscope around his neck.

The fog of confusion lifted. She backtracked through what must have been the last twenty-four hours. The hospital.

The stretcher. The ambulance. The odd man shaking Her.

Bailey.

"B-b—" she started, but her coughing and sputtering interrupted her words.

"Shhh, take it easy. You've been through a lot. Take it easy," the voice reassured as he put a hand on her shoulder. "Take some deep breaths, okay? You're in the hospital. You were found in a snowstorm. Do you remember?"

She carefully nodded, her eyes still focused on his warm face, his gray hair parted to the side.

"You're really lucky you were brought in when you were. Frostbite and hypothermia were setting in, but we've reversed them both. You're going to be okay, Mrs. Kling."

Okay. She was going to be okay.

And then, somewhere in her panging mind, a horror hit her, a thought so terrifying, her breathing intensified. How could she not have thought about this? Where was her head?

She strained to sit up, urgency driving her movements, but the doctor gently pushed her back down.

"Easy does it. You're going to be okay, but you need to recover. Stay put."

"T-t-odd," she muttered, her voice a little louder but still cracking from not being used. "Todd."

"He's alive. He made it."

"Is he okay?" she said, her breathing still labored, the terror still fading.

"He has a long road to recovery. His leg isn't in good shape."

"I need to see him right now." She again tried to get up.

"Listen. I know. I know. But you can't see him right now. He's in surgery."

"What?" Panic elevated in her chest, in her heart again. "Surgery?"

"For his leg. We need to work on his leg so he'll get normal function back. It was severely sprained, and the cold and frostbite didn't help things. We're doing all we can. But the good news is you both survived. He survived, Mrs. Kling. He's going to make it. So you need to focus on your recovery right now. I will let you see him as soon as humanly possible. You need to get some rest, though, okay?"

She took a few more deep breaths, still uncomfortable with not getting to see her husband.

"If you're up to it, you do have a few visitors. I've practically had to bolt the door and get extra security to keep them out, but we needed to make sure you were okay."

Jess smiled. "Thank you. Yes, send them in."

She knew Todd's mom and dad were in the waiting room. Usually, the woman drove her a little batty with her constant advice on everything from trash bag brands to the best way to sprinkle sugar on apple pie. Today, though, Jess couldn't wait to see her in-laws.

They'd made it through the ordeal, had come out the other side. It was a miracle.

The doctor patted her hand, filled out a few things on her chart, and then smiled. "You ready?"

"I think," she said, pushing a button on her bed to increase the incline.

The doctor headed out the door, and within a minute flat,

Mary dashed to Jess's side.

"Oh my goodness," she squealed, tears flying down her face as she leaned in to squeeze her.

Jess didn't fight it. She savored the feel of her mother-in-law's arms, the soft, soapy scent of her, and savored the moment.

"Jesus, Mary, let the girl breathe. She's just been through a near-death. You don't need to suffocate her," Ed said, and Jess laughed.

Mary backed up and Ed stood at her side, both looking down at Jess. "Good to see you, honey," he said, reaching out to pat her hand. "So good to see you."

Mary started crying again, a hand covering her mouth. "If we had lost you two...."

"But you didn't. We're okay." Jess said, reaching to touch Mary's arm. She was anxious to move on to the next most pressing topic on her mind. "How's Henry?"

"He's fine, honey. He was a little bit dehydrated and very depressed when we got to him. We realized on Monday something was wrong because we couldn't get ahold of you. We went to the house straight away. That's when we found him and figured something was wrong. He's been with us since then. He misses you guys, but he's okay."

"I'll say. That horse took over my side of the bed," Ed said, and Mary elbowed him.

Jess didn't know why, but she found this funny. The talk of Henry, the fact that he was okay, the bantering between Ed and Mary.

She was so thankful to see them arguing, bickering, and

just being them. It was beautiful.

"Thank you. Both of you," Jess said, meaning it. Her in-laws were sometimes a lot to take in, especially since she wasn't really used to the interactions of family. Still, they were her family. They were hers. She was glad to get the opportunity to spend more time with them, to appreciate them.

"Honey, we have so much to catch up on, but there's someone else here to see you."

Jess raised an eyebrow quizzically. Her head ached and she was tired, so tired. However, this new information perked her up. "Who is it?"

She couldn't imagine who else would be here. Her principal? One of the neighbors? Who would be here this quickly?

"It's Sam. He's the one who rescued you."

Jess took a minute to mull it over. "He's still here?"

"Yeah. Said he was too shaken up to just leave. He waited here with you guys until we got here, then decided he wanted to see you."

"Send him in," Jess said quietly.

"Are you sure? If you're too tired, I'm sure he'd understand," Mary said, protective instincts kicking in.

"No. I want to see him," Jess said.

"Okay. We'll be right outside. We're not going anywhere."

"You guys should go home and get some rest."

"Not until Todd's out of surgery."

"After that?" she asked. She knew they had to be exhausted.

"After that," Ed promised, winking.

"Love you," Jess said to both of them, meaning it. They smiled before turning to head out the door to send in Sam.

A minute later, a man dressed in jeans and a flannel came trudging through the door. His face was pale with weariness, exhaustion clearly plastered on his bloodshot eyes and stubbled cheeks.

The sheer sight of him, though, was angelic. Jess's eyes involuntarily welled.

"Hi," she said simply through tears.

"Hi," the gruff voice said. He took a seat near her bed. "I'm sorry to bother you. I'm sure you're tired. I just wanted to make sure you're okay."

Jess sat, studying the miracle of a man for a long moment. He wasn't what she'd pictured a miracle to look like. He was a miracle dressed in what was probably a shirt from a cheap department store, steel-toed boots on his feet. He was a man who probably watched football games every weekend and drank a few beers on his nights off. He was a husky man, a warm man. He was a man who reminded her of Todd.

This man, though, was a miracle. He'd saved them. He was nothing short of a hero.

"You're not bothering me," she said seriously. "You saved us. We owe you our lives." Tears started welling again.

"I didn't save you. You two saved yourselves. It's a miracle you survived. I just happened to spot you."

"How? How did you even see us?"

He fiddled with his hands, seeming to contemplate something. "I don't know. I just don't know. I guess I was just meant to find you. I happened to take a wrong turn, to end up that way. I happened to keep driving even after I should've turned around. And I just happened to think I saw something down the embankment. It was a miracle, really."

"Yes, it was. Thank you. Thank you so much." She reached for his hand, squeezing it, staring him directly in the eyes.

"No problem."

The room fell silent again, the rhythmic beeping of the machines hooked to her the only sound echoing.

"I hate to bother you. But can I ask you something?" he asked, seeming hesitant.

"You can ask me anything. Seriously. I think it's the least I can do."

"Who's Bailey?"

Her stomach lurched. She hadn't been predicting that one, had been so absorbed in surviving and the hospital and him that she'd lost sight of Bailey. It made her feel bad.

She looked away from Sam, her tears falling a little more freely now. She inhaled before turning back. "She was my daughter."

"When I found you," he practically whispered, his voice soft with apparent reverence, "you said her name."

Jess nodded, fiddling with her hands now. "I... I was with her when you...."

"You saw her?"

"I know. It sounds crazy. But she was there. It was like a dream. She stood there, reaching out to me. I was so happy. But then... you yanked me back."

Sam ran a hand through his hair. "I'm sorry."

"Don't be. I'm glad. I'm not done here. I know I'm not

done here. It's just.... I feel like I abandoned her. I feel like I could've stayed."

"You're right, though. You're not done here. She knows that."

Jess looked at him. "You don't think I'm crazy?"

"I don't think that at all. I think in times like you were experiencing, all kinds of things are possible."

"I know I was hallucinating. I know that. But it felt so real...."

"I don't think you were just hallucinating," Sam said.

"What do you mean?"

He sighed, paused, and then started talking. "Her name was Rose. She was our firstborn. When she came into this world, she was our everything. Liz and I had only been married two years. She was beautiful, that little girl. Red hair, curls that were out of this world, a laugh to warm you." He beamed, thinking of the memories.

She was silent, sensing he needed to finish.

He continued. "It was a terrible accident. No one's fault, not really. The roads were icy. It had happened so suddenly. We were going so slow, and so was the other car. But in an instant, everything changed. Our world ended as we knew it. We were fine, Liz and I. Rose was gone. Three years old and just gone."

Tears were in his eyes. He wiped them away, the pain clearly still fresh. Jess knew the pain all too well. She reached for his hand.

"I wanted to die. I wanted nothing more than to die. But I didn't. I lived. The years passed, we had another baby, and the pain dulled. It didn't disappear, but it dulled to the point of being survivable. And then it happened. My heart attack. Doctors said I shouldn't have survived. Doctors said I clinically died for a while. That's when I saw her last."

"You mean, you saw her, saw her?"

"I mean, when I was lying on the table, when they were trying to bring me back, I wasn't there. I danced in our garden with my little girl. The rose bushes, the ones she thought were so pretty, were behind us. The sun shone perfectly, the blue sky shimmering. I danced with my little girl, and she laughed and sang. I was so happy, so warmed to be with her again. I wanted to stay forever. But she told me I couldn't. She said I wasn't done, that I'd have to come back another time."

Jess cried again, tears running down her cheeks. She knew the pain. She knew the feeling. "Then what?"

"Then I was here. Back here, alive. Afterward, when I realized what had happened, I was mad for a while. I hated that I'd left her. But you know what? She was right. I wasn't done. Because now look. If I'd been done, you two might not be here right now."

"We *wouldn't* be here," Jess said, swiping at her tears again. "We wouldn't be here."

The words of the hero stranger sat with her, stirred in her.

She knew the next few weeks would be filled with struggles and confusion. She knew she'd go back to those moments time and time again. She knew she'd feel sad, knowing her little girl danced out there without her.

Still, his words soothed.

He wasn't done here. And apparently neither was she.

"Thank you. Thank you for telling the story. It's helped. Thank you for saving me in so many ways," she said, reaching for his hand to squeeze it again.

"My pleasure," he said, reaching down to kiss her hand gently. It wasn't a sensuous kiss of any sort. It was a kiss of understanding, of gratitude.

"Stay in touch," he said. "I've left my number with your in-laws. Call if you need anything, either of you."

"Will do. Now get home to your family. You've done enough saving for one day."

He nodded, stood quietly, and left.

She smiled to herself, though. She'd be okay. She was here. Todd was here.

They were here for a reason.

***

A few hours later, Jess's eyes opened again. She'd apparently drifted off, the surprise and shock coupled with her condition getting to her. It felt good to wake up under blankets.

She sat up slowly, careful not to rip any wires out.

That's when her eyes landed on something, and her heart sputtered.

A bouquet of yellow roses. The same vibrant yellow her baby girl had been holding.

As if on cue, the nurse came through the door to check her vitals.

"Excuse me." Jess pointed at the bouquet on the stand nearby before the nurse could even get her stethoscope out. "What does the card say?"

The nurse smiled, her feet plodding across the waxy floor to retrieve the card. She handed it to Jess, whose hands were shaking.

These were Rose's favorite color. They were in the visit I mentioned. They bring me comfort now. I hope they do the same for you.

Sam.

Jess didn't know if she should cry or laugh.

Yellow. Yellow roses.

It was like Sam had been purposefully sent for them. It was too crazy to be a coincidence.

The yellow roses did comfort her. She was comforted by the fact that Sam understood. She was comforted by the fact that she had survived with Todd.

She was also comforted by the thought that somewhere in the great beyond, two little girls were dancing in a garden of yellow roses, the sunshine gleaming down on them.

***

The nurse wheeled her into the room, and the sight of him assaulted her senses. Her hand instinctually rose to her mouth, holding back her gasp, her sobs.

Todd.

He lay there in his bed, machines hooked up to him. Tears rolled down her face as she moved her hand from her mouth and said his name. He moved his head slightly to better see her. Despite the pain and confusion he was probably feeling, he managed a smile.

The nurse wheeled her over to him. "I'll be back for you in a few minutes. Doctor's orders," the woman said, parking Jess beside Todd's bed. Jess had already stopped listening, her focus on more important things. She reached for Todd's hand, clutching it like she had so many times before. This time, though, it was different.

It was a touch of hope, a touch soothing in its promise of life.

They'd made it. Against all the odds, they'd made it.

Jess had spent hours waiting for this reunion, the thought of being away from Todd killing her. After days in a truck together, after days of thinking they'd die there together, being in another room was unbearable. When Todd had finally come out of surgery and the doctors had agreed to let her visit, she'd practically sprung from her bed and dashed down the hallway herself. She needed him, especially after all they'd been through.

They sat for a while, reveling in the sight of each other. Todd's eyes drooped heavily, grogginess from his surgery still weighing on him. His leg was in worse shape than they'd thought. It would be a long road to recovery.

But they'd made it. They could walk the road together. They had so much left to do, and now they had the chance to do it.

He rubbed her hand with his thumb like he always did.

"We made it," he whispered, probably also reveling in this moment. The beeping machines around them created a less-than-romantic chorus to set the scene. The antiseptic smell mixing with the clinically white walls was no picture-perfect backdrop. Though Jess floated in a sea of romance. It was the most beautiful moment of their love story. It was the moment she realized their love had helped them survive, that together they could beat even the most impossible odds.

"We did." She smiled back before leaning in, resting her head on the bed as close to him as she could, planting a kiss on his hand. "Your mom and dad are here. They're anxious to see you. I should go get them."

He squeezed her hand. "Not just yet. Just a few more minutes. I want to talk to you about something."

He fiddled with her hand, averting his eyes before slowly speaking. "I saw her, Jess."

"Who?" she asked, her stomach falling a bit. She knew what he would say, knew from the tone of his voice he had to be talking about her. He had to be talking about the same thing that was on her mind. He only talked in that voice when he talked about her.

She wasn't sure if she was ready to hear what he had to say. She knew her vision of Bailey hadn't just been a hallucination. But if Todd saw her, too, it would only solidify it even more.

"Bailey. Right before…," he started, and tears came to his eyes. He pressed his thumb and forefinger into the corners of his eye sockets, trying to slow the tears. She pulled his hand down.

"I know. I saw her, too," Jess said, leaning in. Despite the pain in her joints, in her head, she leaned in close enough to whisper, close enough they were nose to nose. "I saw her too.

She's beautiful."

He looked into her eyes, his soulful eyes dancing with the image in his head. He nodded slowly, careful not to taint the moment. For a solid minute, they sat staring at each other, basking in the connection, in the memory, in the knowledge.

They didn't talk about loss or about regret. They didn't talk about afterlife or religion. They didn't talk about what it all meant.

They sat, clutching each other, a man and a woman in love, a man and a woman who had lost so much yet had gained so much back in a strange way. They sat as survivors, as best friends, and as faithfully made believers in fate.

"We have so much left to do here," she said, a smile on her face. No longer was this a scary prospect or an exhausting prospect. It was an exciting one.

"We do." He nodded. "We have so much left to do."

"We have a long road ahead of us first, though," she said, reality creeping back in. He carefully lifted her hand to his lips, planting a kiss on it. His beard tickled her skin, and she smiled. Ignoring the doctor's warnings and all rational thought, Jess slowly gathered the strength to stand and climb into bed with her husband. She gingerly aligned herself as to not hurt his leg, slinking in beside him. This was probably a bad idea, but she didn't care. She needed to be held by her husband, needed his arms around her. She just needed him.

When they were situated and comfortable, she let herself slip slowly toward sleep, the warmth of the bed, of Todd reassuring her she wasn't dreaming. They were okay. They'd made it.

"We're going to be okay. I love you," he murmured into her hair, his hands caressing her.

"I love you too. Until my dying breath," she responded, whispering it into his lips before kissing him.

"Until my dying breath," he said when he pulled away. "Except my dying breath isn't happening today." He smiled and she nodded, leaning into his chest, the warmth of their bodies matching the perfect warmth of their hearts.

Epilogue

Beneath a cluster of trees sits a memorial. There is a wooden cross, crudely shaped from lumber. The cross, pounded into the ground, has weathered many winters now, and the rotting edges and worn state of it seems ill-fitting for its joyous memorial.

It is not, like so many crosses, a memorial for death.

It is a memorial for the living.

Atop the cross, tattered in its own right, is a swatch of red fabric, the very red fabric that redeemed them that freezing week years ago.

***

With the *Little Einstein* CD on repeat, he taps wildly as she rolls her eyes. The sun shimmers down on them, like it usually does on this day. It sometimes feels like it's God's wink at them.

Despite the fact that the road is clear, the sky a crystal blue, her hands tense a little bit on the wheel. They always do here. She can't help it.

They almost lost it all.

Still, things are different than that night. So much is different now.

So much is different, in a way, *because* of that night they almost lost it all. In an odd, terrifying way, that night put them on the road to today, on the road to a life greater than they could've imagined. It had landed them on a path to a life more beautiful than they could've dreamed for themselves when they couldn't see past the snow on the windshield, couldn't imagine surviving the ordeal.

But they had survived. By a miracle, by a wrong turn, by a snowplow driver named Sam, they'd survived.

She pulls off the road onto the shoulder, her hazard lights blinking as a precaution. She takes a lot more precautions these days.

"Are you going to get the basket and Henry?" Todd asks after stopping his horrible rendition of Emma's favorite song. She is giggling wildly in the back seat of the minivan. Henry is in the row behind her, alert as always, waiting to see if his self-appointed charge needs anything.

"Don't I always?" Jessica responds, smiling at him. They begin to unload cautiously, following the routine they've followed for several years now.

They're careful when unloading their precious cargo, even though the road is, like that fateful night, barren. This empty stretch of road is eerie in a way. It's a bit unsettling to be back.

It's different this time, she reminds herself as she grabs Henry's leash and the basket. Todd unbuckles Emma from her car seat, the three-year-old babbling about sunshine and Henry. They cautiously cross the road, treading down the only passable slope of the grassy hill, careful not to tumble down it.

They tread on what feels like sacred ground, four pieces of one family, four pieces of one heart. Their feet amble down the hill, a familiar pathway they've traveled several times before. They make their way down the embankment, down under the trees, their destination in sight.

They spread out the blanket, getting situated, a task never easy with a wriggling child full of life and excitement. Jess hands Emma the yellow rose. The little girl toddles over to the memorial, gently tossing the rose in the same spot as always.

She doesn't understand what this means, Jessica thinks as they settle in for lunch. *Someday, though, someday she will.*

Many call them crazy for this tradition they started a few years ago. Many think it's the lingering effects of the tragedy whirring in their brains that lures them back. Some call it masochistic.

For Todd and Jessica, though, revisiting the scene of their fateful accident is so much more than that.

It's therapeutic. It's significant. It's essential.

They almost lost it all at this spot.

They regained it all at this spot too.

Looking back, she can barely recognize the couple trapped in the storm. Back then, they had been two people who naively thought life lasted forever, that they had so much time. They'd thought they were immortal, their lives irrevocably promised to them.

The accident was so many things for them.

It was a struggle, painful, and terrifying.

But it was also a blessing, a wake-up call, and a reminder.

Their recovery had been tedious. They'd woken up in the hospital confused, scared, alone. Most of all, Jessica had woken up in shock. Surely she wasn't alive. She couldn't be. It had ended for them. They'd said their goodbyes, had resigned themselves to their future. How the hell could they have survived?

Immediately following her initial shock, after she'd processed what had happened, she'd felt dismay. Bailey. She'd seen Bailey, had almost touched her. She was glad to be alive, but she was depressed too. It felt like she'd lost her little girl again.

Still, Sam's words stuck with her. Alive. She'd survived. And, without a doubt, there was a reason for it.

With that, Jessica knew they were getting a fresh start on life. By some miracle, they weren't gone yet. They weren't finished. Although it pained her to say goodbye to Bailey again, she knew within her heart that Bailey would be waiting for her. She knew her little girl would be okay, Todd's grandma and great-aunt looking out for her by the dock. They'd take care of her. For now, she wasn't done here. When Sam had delivered those yellow roses to the hospital, it had only solidified it for her.

Bailey would understand. Bailey would want them to finish out their purpose. And, at the very least, Jess felt comforted by the sight of her little girl in her tutu, happy, safe, at peace. She was relieved to know she was okay, in a happy place where someday Jess would join her.

The road to recovery had been long. Todd had almost lost his leg. The two had endured a gruelingly long hospital stay complete with tests, surgeries, and scary diagnoses. Nonetheless, they'd prevailed. They'd fought their way back to life, back to their love, and back to a sense of normalcy.

Their first task once Todd was in the clear was to take Sam out for dinner. They'd taken their savior, their hero, out along with his wife, Liz. The four had become fast friends and still talked regularly, even to this day. Sam was even Emma's godfather. It only seemed fitting after all he'd done that day to make sure they'd have a future, have a chance to have another child.

Even today, when she thinks about it, she doesn't understand. The wrong turn, his eyes landing in the right spot down the embankment, his reaction. It was nothing short of miraculous. Todd's mom had, in fact, called in a rescue crew, but they'd struggled to find the couple. The helicopter they'd heard during their ordeal had been part of the rescue crew but, with the low visibility, they hadn't spotted the truck. If it hadn't been for Sam, no one would've come back. They would've died underneath those trees.

In all reality, Jessica knows she and Todd should've taken that final journey, should've left this place. They shouldn't be here.

But they are. They are here. And they'd made the most of it once they'd wrapped their heads around it.

Snapping back to the present, Jessica smiles. They unload

the picnic basket, getting Emma's food ready first, of course. They'd learned parenting meant putting others first all the time. They'd learned life was a whole lot bigger than they thought. They'd learned just how grateful they were to survive, to feel this depth of life through the birth of their child.

They'd changed. They'd grown. Most of all, though, they'd lived.

They'd packed more life into the past six years than they'd packed in the first thirty. They'd crossed off their bucket list. They'd spent time with family. They'd soaked in every warm fire, every night on the couch, every cup of hot tea they got their hands on.

It took a devastating dance with death for Jess to realize life is lived in the seemingly small moments, the tiny memories most don't even think about.

Sitting here, the sun beaming down on their backs, she says a silent prayer, a silent thank-you as she does every year, every day in reality. Her fingers find a blade of grass to twirl, the anxiety in her chest floating away at the sight of her family, at the symbolism of a miracle sitting with her.

The silence of the moment seems fitting, as it always does. Their yearly trip here is perhaps ludicrous, perhaps masochistic.

But it is also soothing. It's a reminder to not take life for granted. Even two people who had been to the brink and back sometimes needed to be reminded of that. Between the doctor appointments, work, broken water heaters, and chaotic schedules, even they needed to be reminded of what mattered most.

Life. Love. Their relationship. Emma.

As they do every year, they sit in silent reverie, their minds dancing through the years, through those harrowing moments, through the rescue, through survival.

It is only after an appropriate amount of silent reflection that Todd breaks the silence, that his lips say the words she knows all too well. Her heart flutters at the expectation of them, at what they've come to symbolize.

A life well lived. A life of memories. A life of love, of quite literally surviving against the odds, of gratitude.

A life made together. A life they continue to make together.

Every time he says the words, she can't help but smile, can't help but bask in the reality of the words. They're still here. They're still here to talk about the memories, to walk memory lane.

She reaches for his hand, knowing what's coming. He grins back at her, his thumb rubbing the back of her hand. She nods, egging him on. He pauses in reflection as Emma yammers to Henry about her sandwich and the trees and the sun.

They don't care. The moment is special, reverent, holy.

Todd slowly, meticulously, says the words.

"Do you remember when…?"

Her gaze catches his, and their hearts share in a simultaneous burst of joy, their minds transcending the moment and taking them back, back through a love that survived the unsurvivable.

She squeezes his hand tightly, the warmth radiating between their fingers.

She does remember. She remembers it all. And she wouldn't have it any other way.

Acknowledgements

First and foremost, I want to thank everyone at Hot Tree Publishing for believing in my writing and taking a chance on me. I am so blessed to call myself an author at Hot Tree Publishing. Your dedication to supporting authors' passions and writing is out of this world. Thank you to Becky, Olivia, Justine, Peggy, Claire, and everyone else who has helped in every phase of the process. Thank you for helping me make works I am proud to see on shelves. Thank you to all of the authors in the Hot Tree family for tirelessly supporting one another and creating not just a publishing atmosphere, but a family atmosphere.

Thank you to my readers. When I first started this journey, I didn't know if I'd ever have a single person read my work. Now, to have my books in so many hands, to hear your supportive comments, to see you enjoying my characters—it's nothing short of a dream come true. I am so thankful for everyone who has ever taken a chance on me by buying a book, reviewing one of my books, sharing my works, or just offering me your kind words. Thank you to all of the amazing book bloggers out there who make it possible for authors like me to find a place in the market.

A huge thank-you to my parents and family for all of your support. Thank you to my parents, Ken and Lori Keagy, for instilling a love of books within me at a young age and teaching me to dream big. Thank you, Grandma Bonnie, for always supporting me at every event and sharing my books.

Thank you to my husband, Chad, for going above and beyond to support my passions. From driving three hours to a rained-out book event to wearing your book T-shirts, you're always there for me. You dry my tears when I feel like giving up and tell me to keep going. You celebrate with me when my dreams come true. You are the love of my life, my best friend, and most days, my complete sense of sanity. I love you.

Thank you to all of my friends and coworkers who have gone above and beyond to support my writing. Thank you especially to Dr. Letcher, Christie James, Kelly Rubritz, Alicia Schmouder, Lynette Luke, Jennifer Carney, Kristin Mathias, and all of my other tireless supporters. A huge thank-you goes to Kay Shuma for following me on this journey from book one and always offering me encouragement. On tough days, your kind words keep me going. Thank you for believing in my writing and my characters.

Thank you to my best friend Jamie Lynch. This book came to be after Chad and I drove to the comedy show that snowy, February night. *Remember When* was born on the back roads on the way to Patton. Thank you for always reminding me to live life to the fullest and to chase adventure. Thank you for the beautiful and hilarious memories, even if most do involve bathrooms or nuns.

And of course, thank you to my best buddy, Henry. Our cupcake days, hometown adventures, and spontaneous dance parties around the house help me remember that life truly is about the little moments.